CW00832709

THE FENCE BUSTERS

The open Texas range was the finest cattle-land in the world. But when some forward thinking men erected fences, others suffered the consequences as their cattle were deprived of water and the best grassland. These men turned night-riders, destroying the long fence lines. Lives were lost and property ruined . . . Young and reckless, Tom Midnight joined the ranks of the fencers; his flaming guns were there to argue with the eastern speculators, seeking to fan the flames of conflict.

TOM GORDON

THE FENCE BUSTERS

Complete and Unabridged

LINFORD
Leicester

First published in Great Britain in 1952

First Linford Edition
published 2010

British Library CIP Data

Gordon, Tom.
    The fence busters.- -(Linford western library)
    1. Western stories.
    2. Large type books.
    I. Title II. Series
    823.9'14–dc22

    ISBN 978–1–44480–130–9

Published by
F. A. Thorpe (Publishing)
Anstey, Leicestershire

Set by Words & Graphics Ltd.
Anstey, Leicestershire
Printed and bound in Great Britain by
T. J. International Ltd., Padstow, Cornwall

This book is printed on acid-free paper

1

Five men rode the length of the one street that was Devine, cowtown in Medina County, Texas. The sun was high and their shadows short and black against the near-white of the dusty trail. It was hot, too, and the sweat came down their brown, lean cheeks in rivulets; their shirts showed dark patches where it clung to their perspiring backs.

They came to a rail fronting a bleached and warping frame building that housed among other business a livery stable; only they weren't there to use the stable.

They dismounted, easily and yet with the stiffness of men living a great part of their lives with feet in stirrups. Four men approached a crude door that let into the building next to the livery stable. On it a notice was tacked. It was

1

laconic. It said, 'The Gliddon Barbed Wire Manufacturing Co. — Walter Rath, Rep.'

The fifth squatted on the board walk, a few yards along and hard by the open window of the Gliddon office. And men don't sit in the full glare of an early summer sun when shade is near; not without good reason. This one had a reason. It demanded that he should keep his hand close to the butt of his Colt .45 . . . just in case.

The door stuck when they tried to open it. Ben Coe, leading the party, kicked hard at the bottom and booted it open.

Inside, behind a table that was used for a desk, a small man in ornate waistcoat looked up. He was struggling with a scratchy pen and some muddy ink, trying to compile a letter, and he looked like a man mighty relieved to be interrupted.

He said, affably, in the deep, slow nasal of a Missouri man, 'This ink-well's drier than the state of Mexico.'

And then he saw what was pointing at him.

One of the men had a gun out. Walt Rath, the wire salesman from Missouri, stopped talking abruptly. He always said he felt kinda tongue tied in the presence of Samuel Colt.

Ben Coe, who was plainly leader of the party, caught the flash of gun-metal and rounded on the man. 'Put that gun away,' he rapped. 'This is a deputation, not a gun party.'

'Deputation?' Walt Rath had guts, and he was sarcastic. 'When did citizens of Devine get to includin' professional gunnies like Gun De Leon in their deputations?'

Ben Coe said, briefly, 'Guess he just jined us, comin' down,' and anyone looking closely at him might have thought that he and his companions weren't too pleased about having Gun De Leon join their party — especially weren't too pleased because now he was already toting a gun.

De Leon's thin face went sarcastic.

'The hell, Ben, talkin's no good to these wire pedlars. Let's cut the cackle an' string him up with his own blamed barbed wire.'

'No.' Coe stepped between the gunnie and the little Missouri man. 'We didn't come here to do that. We don't want any more trouble than necessary.'

Little Walt Rath came in quickly with, 'Them's right nice sentiments to hear, Ben.'

But Coe's face didn't soften. His eyes were pin-points of anger in his weather-reddened face. His voice grated, 'We came here for a purpose, Rath. We'll get it over quickly. You're gettin' warned, hombre — get out of town if you want to keep your hide whole. We don't go for fencers an' fencin' — we go even less for wire pedlars. Any guy that sets up office to peddle wire here in Devine is sure choosing an unhealthy location to work in.'

'You're runnin' me outa town?'

'About that. Just now we're givin' you a friendly warnin' — an' that's to save trouble all round, I guess. Get out of Devine today. If you're not out by tomorrow, we'll carry you out.'

'Watch out that bein' carried ain't permanent,' De Leon said, and the threat implied was unmistakable.

Walt Rath's eyes narrowed thoughtfully, looking at the lean gunman with the ornamented Colt butts. He wasn't bothered by Coe and his three companions; they were decent men whose existence appeared to be threatened at the moment by any fencing of the range and accordingly they were fighting back against the menace. But the professional gunman was a different proposition. And lately there'd been quite a few gunnies like De Leon drift into Devine.

He said, levelly, 'What stake have you got in this fencebustin', De Leon? You ain't got no land. What's it add up to, anyway?'

De Leon sneered, 'I jes' hate the guts of all fencers, that's all. And I'm the kind that fights what I hate, see?'

5

But Walt Rath shook his greying head. 'Your kind never fights without something bein' behind it. I got an idea maybe someone sent you to Devine to stir up trouble. That's your trade, ain't it, Gun?' he ended softly.

De Leon didn't answer. His lips twisted in contempt. Then Ben Coe stirred. He dragged his eyes reluctantly away from the man who had tacked himself on to their party — almost it seemed as though there was a question in them. And that question might have been — 'Could Walt Rath be right? Was De Leon stirring up trouble here in Devine?'

'We'll go,' he announced shortly. 'You've been warned, Rath. We won't stand for wire pedlars right here in Devine. Get out while the goin's good.'

'An' what about the people who want wire?' asked Rath. 'Don't they count?'

'They won't want wire when they see what we're gonna do to it all,' Coe grated. 'Any wire that goes up will be cut down. Who's gonna buy when things are like that?'

Rath came round his table as they turned to leave. He said, earnestly, 'You're makin' a big mistake, fellars. Wire'll be the makin' of Texas. Some day you'll find that wire's what you need yourself — '

'Maybe. But we've got along fine without it until now, an' I opine we can get along without it for some time longer.' Coe opened the door. The man along the sidewalk rose, seeing them. He hadn't been necessary, after all. Perhaps he seemed relieved not to have had to use his gun. A lot of these fence busters were pretty good men and didn't like unnecessary gunplay.

Walt Rath called from the door. 'Another mistake, Coe, is for you an' your friends to get in cahoots with paid trouble-makers like De Leon. They're usin' you — '

Rath never finished the sentence. De Leon came round quicker than lightning. His face was expressionless, except for the eyes which showed deep satisfaction. Then his gun flashed in a descending arc, and the Missouri man was struck down right in his doorway.

Coe shouted, 'You didn't need to do that.' And there was that nasty doubt in his mind as he spoke. He was wondering, was it true what Rath had hinted — that someone was paying men like De Leon to stir up trouble here in Devine? He was an uneasy, unhappy deputation leader right at that moment.

De Leon snapped, 'I don't take talk like that from no man.'

Coe's narrowed eyes probed deep into the gunman's soul, and what he saw there he didn't like. 'You enjoy violence, don't you, Gun?' he said softly. 'You like swingin' a gun and feelin' it smack on to someone's skull. I guess you like the thrill of shootin' a man, too, don't you?'

De Leon braced, legs apart. 'Could be,' he said, then saw that Coe's companions were ready to go for their guns. The odds were against him, and professional gunmen don't fight against odds. He scowled.

Coe told him point-blank, 'I've got doubts about you, Gun. Maybe Rath was right in what he said. Well, we're fightin' against the fencers because we guess we'll go under if they split up the land. Understand that? We're fightin' for our existence. Ef we find someone's making money out of raisin' trouble, we won't like it, *sabe*?'

De Leon understood. He walked away. He was thinking it wasn't as easy as it sounded, getting men to fly at each other's throats.

One of the Texans started to drag Walt Rath into the shade of his office. 'Guess he ain't hurt much,' he opined. 'No more'n a kick from a cow, I reckon. He'll be all right in a few minutes.'

They went out and left him. As they rode down the street they passed a jaded prospector with a laden donkey. He called, 'It ain't same, up 'mong the hill trails. Thar's Injuns on the move agen. They're talkin' big pow-wow an' gatherin' around Wichita for another

9

war agen the white man, dog blast 'em all.'

Riding on, Ben Coe had a sudden thought that a lot of fences would be useful during Indian raids. Cattle could be collected the more easily and driven to safer pastures, say. Abruptly he wrenched away from the thought. He didn't want to give any credit to wiring the range. To date he had suffered too much from it.

*　*　*

The boss looked at Walt Rath. The wire pedlar's head was bandaged, and his face pale, but much of his old jauntiness was back. They were in the Gliddon offices over in San Antonio, capital of Bexar County. They were good offices; they had proper desks, chairs that were padded, and bright, shiny new cuspidors. In Bexar County, anyway, barbed wire sales were good and profitable.

Walt said, 'I'm gettin' too old to stick

my nose into places as tough as Devine. You need someone younger, tougher. Someone who can fight back.'

'You've always been a fighter, Walt,' the boss said.

'Sure, but the years catch up on you.' Walt Rath had made his decision. 'I'm not the man for that job, boss. Sure I'll go back, but — find a man to take over from me pretty quickly. I guess I can't stand that town much longer — or it can't stand me.'

The boss paced the room unhappily. 'We can sell barbed wire by the tens of thousands of miles in Medina County and westwards — that is, if they'll drop this opposition to fencing off the range. Walt, the prize is too big. We've got to go on selling our wire and try to break the opposition to it somehow.'

'That means just what I said. Find yourself a salesman who can fight back. I'm just an agein' old fellar right out of his depth, I guess,' said greying Walt Rath humorously.

11

'Find the man for me, then. You got any ideas?'

Walt Rath paused. 'Only one. The man I'd like to get to succeed me is my nephew. He's just a roamin', no-good puncher right now, an' I'd sure like to see him settled in a job that'll bring him comfort in his old age.'

The boss said, 'This job would. He could make a fortune out of it.'

Walt Rath took out his plug of Honeydew and bit off a chew. 'I've had that in mind a good while,' he admitted. 'An' Tom would do. He's got brains, an' he's a born leader when he chooses. He was an Indian fighter, and did good work in the Mexican war. Oh, he's a fine, big, tough fightin' man, is big Tom Midnight.'

'Midnight?' The boss looked surprised. 'That's not his real name, surely?'

'It's the one his father gave him,' said Walt dryly. 'Though that's not to say his father didn't make it up hisself. We used to tell his paw that after he'd married my sister. He never would say a word on the subject, though, an' our guess was that he'd picked up the name along some of the hoot-owl trails. Maybe he wanted to forget something when he took that name — maybe his real name. But he was a good man to his wife and son, so we won't hold that agen him.'

The boss said, 'All right, try Tom Midnight. Get him to take on the job. Where is he?'

He saw Rath's face twinkle with amusement. 'Where's Tom? Last I heard on him he was in jail up Silverstone way. Something to do with throwin' a sheriff out of his bed, one night, him an' some other rannies. Hell, boss, it was nothin' serious. Just high spirits, I reckon. Just what we want for this kinda job.'

The boss nodded. 'Maybe you're right. Okay, send for him. Meantime you go to Devine an' keep that office open.'

2

In due course a message came to Walt to say that his nephew would visit him just as soon as he had finished breaking in some colts for his late enemy, the Sheriff of Silverstone. There was a postscript to say it was against his principles to visit a blamed fencer, but he'd be kind to an old man.

Two days later Big Tom Midnight wandered casually into the town, forgot why he had come there, and went back of the Hayride Saloon to watch a fight that had flared up between a couple of cattlemen. Word got back to Walt Rath in his dingy little office, who promptly clapped on his hat and frock-coat — twin symbols of a respectable salesman — and went round to find his erring nephew.

Back of the big, excited crowd he asked someone. 'What's the fight about, pardner? Too much liquor, eh?'

The man growled, without turning. 'Too much o' this doggoned wire, more like. Will Addason's gone an' declared he's fer fencin', and that's gonna cut off the Sweet Water Wells from other men's cattle. So one of 'em's goin' for Will right now, I reckon.'

Cunningly, Walt asked, 'You know what kinda wire Addason's figgerin' on usin, pardner? Plain or — barbed?'

It was an incautious question, for it brought round the head of the spectator, and he saw who it was. The spectator opened his mouth to say something, at which moment a savage howl rose from the crowd to announce the fall of one of the fighters.

It seemed to be the end of the fight, for at once the crowd began to spill away from the tight knot they had formed, and start the short trek back to the Hayride Saloon. Walt didn't want to go that way, but the pressure of the crowd forced him along with them. Then, just by the back door of the saloon, little Walt Rath felt a hand, heavy and pregnant with menace, grip into his shoulder — found himself being turned.

The man who had recognised him in the crowd was holding him now, holding him and shouting, 'Hey, keep back, fellars. We got another fencer hyar, the King Rattler hisself, I guess.'

The crowd was all shouting, swaying as excited crowds always do, and getting more uproarious every second. Then it parted, and a man with a bleeding, battered face came through dragging along an older man in much worse condition.

Walt thought, 'They're the couple who've been fightin'.' Then he recognised the older man and thought, 'That's Addason — and he looks bad.' The old man stood there swaying, his eyes glazed and vacant, his torn lips apart as his jaw sagged from weakness.

Walt glanced at his opponent. It took him seconds before he recognised him.

16

Then the man opened his mouth and the familiar voice brought back memory. It was Stan Copey, known as the 'Longhorn', because he held many of the physical characteristics of the celebrated Texan steer.

And he was a bully, for ever looking for trouble.

The Longhorn shouted, 'I done fer one blamed fencer today, now I'll do fer the other!' The hair, black and coarse, was matted into the blood of the Longhorn's face, making him so savage in appearance that even the stout-hearted Missourian quailed.

It was at that moment that Walt Rath spotted his nephew in the crowd. He wasn't hard to spot, because in a land of big men Tom Midnight was still inches taller than his fellows.

He came pushing to the edge of the crowd. There was a little smile on his lips, but he seemed to be watching and calculating. Walt pulled his captor towards his nephew.

'For Pete's sake get me outa here,

Tom,' he gasped. 'These fellars mean trouble.'

Midnight grinned down at him and couldn't resist saying, 'You blamed old fencer, you got yourself to thank for this.'

Some of the crowd nearby heard and laughed, and it made little Walt Rath hopping mad. 'Goddamit, Tom, this ain't no time for foolin' — ' he gasped.

But Midnight wasn't looking at him now. He was looking to where old Will Addason stood swaying, eyes glazed and unseeing. Abruptly he stepped forward.

It was at the moment that the Longhorn came milling in at the little Missourian. It was what the Longhorn liked — a big crowd shouting their heads off, while he pounded some weaker man to jelly. He had done it often, and few men chose voluntarily to fight against the Longhorn. The Longhorn used fists until it suited him to resort to feet, but if required he swung a gun, too. He was just one big bad man, in most people's estimation.

He was all that and more in Walt Rath's mind as he came charging across. Old Will Addason got in the way and spun round before falling heavily. He didn't move, once on the ground, and there was a danger that the crowd would trample on him.

Walt spun aside desperately as the Longhorn charged, so that the first blows missed him completely. And that made the Longhorn mad. He jumped in, far more quickly than you'd have thought his bulk allowed, grabbed Walt and proceeded to beat him about the head — the head that had suffered enough, this last week or so.

Then, unexpectedly, Walt found himself released. He staggered back into the crowd and realised that it was suddenly, expectantly silent. Then he realised why.

Big Tom Midnight had pulled the Longhorn away. The Longhorn wasn't used to such treatment and started to shout his anger, but Midnight didn't seem bothered. He was crossing to kneel by the side of old Will Addason; one glance and he was up, shouting, 'This old-timer's pretty bad. I guess he should be put to bed an' a doctor sent for.'

But the Longhorn had other ideas. He was not to be pushed aside so contemptuously before a throng. He came across and took a handful of shirt just under Big Tom's chin, and he snarled, 'I don't let no green guys lay hands on me, stranger.'

Tom squinted down at the rough brown hands that held him. Walt Rath waited for the explosion, because he had seen his volcanic young nephew in action several times. There was that tightening of the muscles of the jaw, the hunching of his shoulders, as though he were flexing his biceps.

But, curiously, he didn't explode. Not immediately. Instead he said, coldly, contemptuously, 'If you don't take them dirty paws off'n me right away, Longhorn, I'll bat you on your thick skull so goddamned hard, your teeth'll be growin' in your boots.'

Longhorn kicked. Big Tom took it on the shin without visible sign of discomfort.

And then he did just as he had said.

As quick as a skittish mare lashing out, his two hands raised above his head, then descended a-top the Longhorn's matted skull. Only, when they came into contact they were two rock-like fists.

The Longhorn staggered under the weight of the blow and some teeth flew out. Then the blood came pouring from his mouth, and someone in the crowd shouted, 'He's bitten his tongue!'

The Longhorn walked round the circle of spectators, racked with the pain of that injured mouth, while Big Tom Midnight rotated slowly to keep him in view. Then the Longhorn charged in suddenly, head down, blood dribbling from his open mouth.

Tom side-stepped and clumped him yet again on top of his skull. The crowd shouted with delight, but Walt Rath could sympathise with the staggering Longhorn. He knew what a sore head felt like.

Next time, the Longhorn came jumping in with fists flying. So Midnight jumped forward to meet him, took a hold on him somewhere between his legs . . . and the next second the Longhorn was flying through the air over the heads of the first ring of spectators.

Big Tom stooped over the inert Will Addason. 'Give us a hand to lift the old boy,' he ordered his uncle.

Walt Rath got indignant and rapped, 'Who the heck are you givin' orders to, you young hellion?' Then he got the nod from young Midnight and understood. The crowd parted for them as they carried the limp body inside. They were cheering still, and patting Midnight's broad shoulders as he came through.

Walt thought, 'My god, if I could get him to work for us! This crowd loves a scrapper, an' I reckon they're no different from all the rest of Texas at that. He'd get results this boy.'

On the edge of the crowd Midnight got impatient and said, 'The hell, you're gettin' old. Here, give him to me,' and he swung Addason up into his arms easily and strode off. Walt watched him go, then went back to his own office. He guessed that this time his big young nephew would get around to seeing him.

An hour later Tom Midnight came lounging into the little room. Walt had his feet up on the table. Midnight elaborately dusted a chair and blew on it, then settled down with his big spurred boots on the table also.

Walt encouraged, 'Sure, go ahead an' make yourself comfortable.'

There was a lazy humour in those blue eyes opposite him. 'That's mighty considerate of you, Uncle, mighty considerate.'

Walt Rath snapped, 'More considerate than you were, back at that fight.

The heck, what did you mean by callin'
me a blamed old fencer publicly, when I
was askin' you to help me?'

'Now, Uncle,' soothed the puncher,
'what good would it have done to have
said, 'Hyar, Uncle Walt. You sure look
to be in a right mess, don't you?' It'd a
done no good at all. Besides, you are a
blamed old fencer, aren't you?'

Walt Rath swung his feet down, but
Midnight just went on drawling, 'Hold
your hosses, Uncle. I didn't get you into
that trouble, but I sure got you out of it.
Don't I get no gratitood?'

Then suddenly he demanded, 'Now,
Walt Rath, tell me why you had me trail
all the way from Silverstone to see you?'

Walt instantly became a salesman. He
said, soothingly, 'You're my favourite
nephew, son, an' you know it. An' all
these years I've felt sad 'cause my dead
sister's boy's been just another cow-
puncher. Okay, now I'm gonna do
somethin' for you, boy. How d'you like
me to make your fortune?'

Midnight watched him through lazily

closed eyes. After a few seconds' silence he said, contemptuously, 'Axle grease, that's what it amounts to! I'm your favourite nevvy 'cause you only got but one, an' I don't see as there's anything'd make you sad except maybe losin' a bit o' business. As for makin' my fortune — '

Walt stopped being a salesman, as he should have done in the beginning. Instead he said, quietly, 'There, I'm not kiddin', Tom. I can make your fortune for you.'

'Peddlin' wire?'

'Peddlin' wire. Some day they're gonna take up this invention of Gliddon's in a big way out here on the range, and when that happens the county representative will make so much money it'll sicken him. Boy,' he said earnestly, 'it's the most wonderful opportunity, an' I'm givin' it to you.'

Midnight promptly came back with — 'Why don't you make *your* fortune, then?'

'Because,' said his uncle simply, 'I'm

a sensitive man. I can't stand people bendin' gun-barrels across my head more'n once. Maybe it's the age that's gettin' into my bones. I reckon this business needs someone bigger, younger, more virile and a whole lot tougher.'

Midnight rose to his feet. 'You're a nice uncle to have,' he said admiringly. 'Just offerin' me a job where they bend gun-barrels across your head.'

Walt stood up anxiously. He came to about his nephew's chin. He said, 'Your answer?'

'I don't like wire pedlars, an' I don't like anyone connected with fencin' at all,' his nephew said bluntly.

'I know what you think about fencing,' said Walt. 'I know, because that's how I felt myself, one time. But I don't think like that any more. I used to think that fencing was a bad thing, but now I see that it's got to come and when it does come it'll be the better for everyone in the farming an' cattle-raisin' business.'

'It'll be good for Gliddon's dividends,'

said young Midnight laconically, and tried to get past. Walt got in the way again.

He said, roughly, 'You're talkin' about somethin' you know nothin' about, Tom. You've got to have fences if you're gonna grow crops, just to keep the cattle out. An' Texas must raise crops, else these new immigrants who're pourin' into the country will starve. An' also, you've got to have fences if you want to raise a better breed than the longhorn, because otherwise you'll just get the longhorn bulls in among your pedigree cows an' ruin 'em.'

'Son, there are a hundred good reasons why the range should be fenced, an' only a few agen it. Just now it's just doggoned prejudice that won't give it a trial — that's why as fast as someone fixes up a fence along comes a party to try to bust it. They don't know why they do it, in many cases, 'cept for cussedness.'

Midnight said, slowly, 'You ever been

up Crossflats way?' His uncle shook his head. 'Well, up Crossflats each fenced off that land that belonged to 'em. When it was done they found that two ranches had all the water, and half a dozen hadn't any. They lost so much cattle, in the end they nearly had to give their land away — to the owners of the waterholes. Now you see why I don't like fencin'.'

Walt Rath said, 'I know it sometimes hurts someone, but you tell me any good innovation which pleases everyone. There never has been any. Without fencing, good grassland becomes over-grazed, and in time that means it'll turn to dust and desert and then everyone's lost out.'

Midnight lifted him off his feet and sat him on the edge of the table. 'Free range, that's what I like,' he said humorously. 'I like it as it's always been, where a man can turn his cattle loose an' round 'em up a coupla times a year an' forget 'em in between.'

From the edge of the table Walt Rath

said, 'All right, you doggoned mule. But don't come whinin' to me you've changed your mind, because I'll get me another man to do this job, you see if I don't.'

But his heart was heavy, because he couldn't think of any man half so good as this fine young nephew of his, now striding away up the boardwalk towards the Hayride Saloon.

3

Late that same afternoon Walter Rath's fashionable San Antonio-made boots were up on the table edge again. He was picking his nails with a bowie knife, when the door was kicked open. Without lifting his head, he said, 'I kinda recognise that door-openin'.'

Gun De Leon was there, and with him two friends. Crafty Walt Rath looked through the bush of his eyebrows and saw them and saw that Gun De Leon hadn't bothered to come in with a gun out, though his hand was ready to dive for it.

De Leon said, 'You were told to leave town.'

Walt looked at him levelly and said, 'I went. I also came back. Now what're you gonna do about it?'

De Leon didn't like that tone and his face darkened with anger. 'This time we'll run you outa town — an' maybe you won't have the legs to bring you back again,' he snarled, and took a pace forward.

Walt rapped, 'Hold up, there. Before you start anythin', tell me — who's payin' you to do this?'

De Leon stopped abruptly. 'Payin' me?' he repeated.

'Sure, that's what I said.' For a little man, facing three armed adversaries and unpleasant men at that, Walt Rath was a cool customer. He said, bitingly, 'You, you Border scum, you never owned a cow, so why have you got to interfere in this fence-war? That fellar that came the other time — Ben Coe, wasn't it? He'd got cause to bellyache. He got shut off the best grassland when they fenced up his way, didn't he? All he's got now is scrub that don't support a cow an acre. He's got some right to feel mad, I reckon, an' I don't hold it agen him, though he did pick the land he's got when he first came to Texas, didn't he? He could have gone farther — '

One of the men suddenly said, 'The mouth he's got! Let's shut it for him, Gun!'

Gun snapped out of his amazement at hearing himself insulted in such a situation. He snarled, 'Scum? Was that what you called me, you barbed-wire pedlar?'

His hand went streaking down to his gun.

Walt Rath calmly splayed his elegant San Antonio-made footwear and fired with the gun that had been resting on his legs every moment that he'd been back in his tiny office.

It's always a lucky shot when you hit, firing from such an angle. Walt aimed plumb for De Leon's stomach, to get the broadest target; he wasn't aiming for any fancy shooting because if it didn't come off he wouldn't ever get a second chance.

As it was, the gun must have pulled a little, and the bullet dug out a big chunk just under De Leon's ribs. A few more inches and he wouldn't even have hit the man and Walt felt a shock that his aim was so bad.

De Leon's face came contorting into pain, and the hand that was diving for the gun never got there, but came hastily across to clasp the injured side.

Like an aggressive bantam cock, little Walt Rath, the fighting Missourian, swung down his feet and stood up, and the twin-barrelled Derringer came round to cover the other men.

Walt said, 'Why don't you do somethin'? You're sure to win. There's only one more round in this gun an' two of you to get it.' Neither puncher moved; they watched that small friend of the gambling man, the Derringer, as though it were a snake. So Walt started to come round the table, saying, mockingly, 'You ain't got the sand, huh?'

He kicked De Leon's gun to one side, then came across to pull out the other men's heavy Colts. De Leon started to swear. Walt said, 'Shut your mouth, you cawing crow, or you'll get this second bullet!' He got the guns out, threw them on to the table, then walked across to De Leon. He wasn't humorous now.

'You cheap kite,' he said. 'I knew if I came back you'd come to bust my head open again. That's why I came back, only this time I never moved from my small friend here. I don't like bein' busted over the head,' he said softly. 'Maybe you'd like to know what it feels like?'

The other men were back against the wall, facing the window. They were helpless with that gun waving across at them; but the way they stood crouched, Walt Rath knew they were ready to spring and bear him down the moment he forgot caution.

De Leon said, 'The hell, you wouldn't bust a wounded man across the head, would you?'

And Walt said, with satisfaction, 'Sure I would — an' enjoy it. The hell, you didn't worry none about slappin' me with that gun o' yourn, did you?'

34

Then he repeated his question of a minute ago, and his voice was steely hard and determined. 'I want to know who's payin' you to spread trouble to us wire salesmen. You tell me, or by god I'll smack you over the head just as you smacked me!'

And De Leon knew he meant it, too.

Then Walt saw that three pair of eyes were focused over his shoulder and knew that he had made a miscalculation in regard to the strength of his enemies. He had. There was the man who was always posted outside when De Leon went to make social calls.

Walt started to throw himself backwards and sideways as he turned towards the window. He was in time to see someone rein up in the street outside, two people on a horse — one a girl. But a gun was much nearer, and an eye peered round the edge of the window.

There was no glass to break. The bullet chipped a bone in Walt Rath's shoulder and sent his turning motion

into a fast-revolving teetotum. He lost
his balance and crashed into a corner.
He didn't know where his Derringer
fell; all he knew was that his hands were
empty and the three disarmed punchers
were diving for their guns.

De Leon was shouting, 'Leave the
son of a wart-hog to me,' and was
grabbing for his gun, when a Colt's
heavy bark sounded from the street
outside. The gunman outside the
window shouted with pain and alarm as
his .45 dropped into the room from a
hand that was smashed and bloody;
then he seemed to fall away. Bullets
were screaming in through the window,
knocking great gouts out of the
boarding of the rear wall.

De Leon saw a man slip off his horse,
then bang it to send it rearing down the
street. There was a girl on a horse,
sitting side-saddle because of her long
skirt. She didn't get into a panic, but
just grabbed for the reins and fought
the panicky beast to a standstill down
the street.

But De Leon was watching the man who had opened fire on them. He was a very big man, and he guessed it would be this hombre Midnight about whom the saloons were talking . . . some said he was related to Walt Rath on the floor.

The big hombre came loping across, two guns swinging up again to belch flame. De Leon heard the scream of lead, heard the tearing sound as wood tore off in strips, and decided that this flimsy office was no protection at all.

He and his men went out of a side-door, running, then got out of the building along a passage that ended where the negro boys were cleaning down the horses from the livery stables. After a minute they realised that no one was after them. Big Midnight hadn't bothered to chase them; they didn't know it, but he was more concerned about the safety of his horse — and the girl upon it.

He picked up his uncle, looked at the wound critically, and then said in surprise, 'Real blood, goldarn it. They always said a fencer only had water in his veins — sour water, too.'

Walt Rath went slowly across to his chair and slumped in it. He looked ill. His nephew said softly, 'There were four of 'em, jumped you, eh?'

'I got one. I thought there were only three, but some lousy buzzard musta been standin' outside, an' he got me.' Then he added thoughtfully, 'Reckon I should be thankin' you for comin' just then, Tom, boy. That De Leon fellar was sure set on exterminatin' me when you arrived.'

Midnight said, 'Old man, this town's too rough for you. It's time you went and got yourself senile in some ceevilised place like San Antonio, where the gals wear hats all the time an' not just on Sundays.'

Walt looked at him. He knew his nephew and knew there was something behind his words. He said, tiredly, 'You get me someone to sell my barbed wire an' I'll go — gladly. As you say, reckon

I'm too old for party games now.'

Big Tom Midnight looked hard at his dusty chaps and then made an astonishing speech. He said, 'Guess I'd better take that job. I don't want it, but I guess I need more'n a puncher's pay from now on.' His blue eyes came up and held his uncle's. There was no embarrassment in them; they were as calm as ever. Big Tom Midnight didn't ever give a hang what people thought. He said, 'You see, Uncle, I been and got myself an orphan to look after. That's why I'm a-takin' this job.'

Walt Rath said, 'What? You've adopted an orphan? What'n Hades — Where d'you find this kid?'

Midnight shoved back his soiled stetson. Even he seemed rather puzzled by the position in which he now found himself. 'Remember poor old Will Addason? When I left you this mornin' I went back to the Hayride Saloon, where I'd put him on a couch. Well, when I got back I found the poor old fellar had croaked. No one was takin' any notice of him, so I thought I'd drive his body home. I thought he might have a wife, and wives get tidy-minded, I guess, and just nacherly hate the idea of husbands' bodies lyin' around.'

'So you took it home?' There was affection in Walt Rath's eyes. This was the kind of boy he would have liked for a son — a man who could cheerfully hold his own against the best, and yet when the time came showed proper feeling.

Tom nodded. 'Guess someone else oughta done it, me being' more of a stranger round these parts than them. But I found Will's buggy, an' someone told me where his ranch lay, so I went off.' He paused, as if thinking of the moment, then said, 'I couldn't have done it, if I had known. It's only a nester's place, an' he didn't have many people to mourn him He didn't have no wife — just a few Mexican an' negro hands . . . and a daughter.'

'You've adopted Will Addason's daughter?' Walt Rath's voice was incredulous.

'What the heck do you know about gals, Tom?'

Tom Midnight said simply, 'There warn't anythin' else I could do. She was just a-cryin' out her eyes all over the place, so I helped a Mex bury her old man, an' then I got up on my hoss to come back to Devine. She wouldn't let me go. Because I'd bothered to bring back the old man she seemed to think I was the only straight fellar in the county. She said she wasn't stayin' there alone; she said she daren't, just with those hands for company.'

Walt said abruptly, 'She was doggone right. The hell, if word had got around she was alone out there, she'd soon have had people poppin' in on her — and not nice people.'

'That's how I figgered it.' Midnight was crossing to the door. 'She's a mighty fine-lookin' gal, an' I was damned if I was goin' to leave her to the buzzards.'

He was opening the door. Walt was saying, 'But you, adoptin' a kid, Tom!

You don't know what you're letting yourself in for — '

And the kid heard. Only it wasn't a kid that walked in through the doorway. It was a tall, straight, pleasant-faced young lady in her early twenties. Just now her eyes were reddened as from weeping, but she still looked good in that office in spite of the marks.

Big Tom grinned. 'Meet my orphan, Uncle. See what I adopted.' Not even a comely young woman could shake his assurance.

Walt sprang to his feet, then winced as his shoulder gave him pain. He said, 'Do take a chair, Miss Addason — if my nephew will dust it for you.' And then he sat back, white-faced from the movement, and pressed a handkerchief over the wound.

The girl was concerned, and forgot her own troubles at sight of Walt's. She pulled off her serviceable, work-worn gloves and came round to Walt's side, saying, 'Let me look.' And when she saw it she upbraided Big Tom Midnight.

'This wound must be painful,' she stormed. 'Your uncle should be put to bed and have a doctor, yet you stand around as casually as if nothing had happened to him.' She was forming a pad with the handkerchief, and then she strapped it across Walt's shoulder, using his smart new San Antonio tie for the purpose.

Walt tried to keep the pain from his face, and grinned at his nephew. He cracked, 'Your orphan child doesn't seem to have much respect for her adopted daddy.'

The girl, flushed from the exertion in that stifling little office, declared, 'No one's adopting me. I wanted to get out of the old homestead quickly, and Tom gave me a lift, that's all.'

The big puncher took out his makings and started to roll a cigarette. He didn't look at his uncle as he asked, 'It wouldn't be safe for a lone gal to stay out on a backwoods farm — you said so yourself, old-timer, didn't you? Okay, now you tell me how much safer she'll be here in this one-eyed cattle town without someone to look after her?'

Walt said to the girl, 'Ain't you got no relatives you could stay with?'

She looked downcast and dejected, suddenly conscious of her loss. 'We came from Tennessee a few years back when mother died. We came overland, and I guess we left all the people we know somewhere in the Appalachians. Not that we had many after the Indian wars.'

Walt looked again at the loungers under the projecting roof of the Hayride, and his brow was worried. He was a decent man and didn't hold with rowdyism where women were concerned, but he guessed he was in the minority in that tough, two-gun town on the Neuces River.

So he said slowly, 'Miss Addason, this town's too rough for a lone gal. If you can't leave it, I guess you'll have to get yourself looked after by someone who c'n stand up to trouble when it comes along.'

'Meanin',' drawled Midnight, 'you gotta get yourself adopted.' He swung his long legs astride a chair and sat with his hat shoved back and his chin resting on the top of the chair. His voice was, as always, gently good-humoured, but there was a note of irony in it now. 'Me,' he said, 'I worked all that out long ago, comin' in down the trail. That's what I meant by sayin' I was adoptin' a gal. Someone's got to look after her, so I figger I might just as well do it myself.'

The girl turned. She looked down at the big puncher and her good-looking face softened. She said, 'You say everything casually and make light of what you do, but — you're a good sort, Tom.' Impulsively she reached out and touched him on the shoulder.

Midnight smiled back, and then his voice drawled, 'Sure I am. You wouldn't believe the sacrifices I'm makin' to adopt you. I've now got to give up movin' around from place to place, I guess; now I'll have to take on this salesman's job, and that means bein' tied to this blamed office.' He swung to his full six-foot-odd height, so that his brow was on a level with the brass tank of the hanging lamp 'I guess I'd better get started right now, 'cause I ain't got much money, I reckon.'

The girl turned her back and lifted her skirt for a moment. The next she was pushing some money into Midnight's hand, saying, 'It's silly, all this talk about having to work to keep me. I've still got the farm. It should give me enough to live on, though I guess I'll be happier doing work while I'm in Devine.'

Walt Rath walked haltingly towards the door. He felt sick with pain, but even so there was a considerable satisfaction in his heart. He could see that he had succeeded in getting his big, battling young nephew to succeed him as field salesman for the Gliddon corporation.

They came out with him, and Tom Midnight helped him along with a strong right arm. Walt said, 'Miss

Addason, if you want work, why don't you ask Mr. Midnight for a job? He'll be out all day gettin' orders, and once they start a-rollin' in he'll need someone to manage this office for him. Very soon now it's goin' to be a mighty important job.'

The idea pleased the girl, he could see. But he also saw that his nephew understood what was behind the suggestion. He was no fool, that big scrapper — he knew Walt Rath was trying to domesticate *him*, Tom Midnight, so that he would go on holding down the job.

And that was nearly Walt Rath's last thought on earth. The next moment he was toppling to the boards of the side-walk with his chest smashed, and Big Tom Midnight was lunging towards the corner of a building where a smoking rifle-barrel protruded.

4

The girl screamed, 'Watch out, Tom!' For Colts — even a pair of .45s — aren't a match for a rifle with any great distance between the contestants. Then she fell on her knees beside the stricken man; she saw that he hadn't long to live and perhaps he knew it.

And then they heard a volley of shots in the distance They were all .45s.

Walt Rath spoke his last. 'Watch Tom . . . he's a good . . . boy . . . ' And then the game little Missouri man was still for ever.

People came pressing closer, looking down in hushed awe, as people always do in the presence of death. Then Midnight came back, pushing his way through the throng.

He knelt by the body, and removed his sweat-stained hat. There didn't seem to be any emotion on his face or in his voice as he spoke. 'They didn't oughta done that to him. I guess he was a pretty good man, Walt Rath — a good neighbour.' He rose to his feet, dusting his knees, and his voice was casual as he said, 'Guess I'd better shoot the varmint that did this. I never did like a galoot who shoots at a man unawares.'

Someone among the crowd pressing round called, 'It was that young hellion, Gun De Leon, did it.'

Without looking up, Midnight said, 'Thanks, neighbour. That's what I wanted to know — he got away afore I could see more'n his tail.' He looked round the circle of faces, and his own was hard and set as he said softly, 'I reckon De Leon'll have friends among you. Okay, they can tell him I'm a-gunnin' for him from this day on. What's more, I'll get him for this!'

Then Midnight seemed to relax with a sigh. He turned and smiled softly at the girl beside him and said, 'Guess you'd better fix yourself down at

Palmer's Hotel while I dispose of old Walt.'

She turned to go, then said, 'Aren't you going to tell the sheriff?'

'No. This is a personal matter. Sher'fs are only good for jailin' drunks, I reckon, not for bringing in killers like De Leon.'

She walked away, her head drooping, while Midnight lifted his uncle and took him away to the burial lot outside the town. All her life Alexandra Addason had been used to sudden death, but twice in one day was over much for her. She went to the small, drab, temperance hotel and wept her heart out on her bed.

After a while she got to feeling very low, because that faded, poorly furnished room would have depressed anyone; so then she bathed her face in the tepid water provided, tidied herself, and went in search of Tom Midnight. He was the only person she knew who could be depended on, she thought.

He was in the office, feet up on the

table, whittling away at a stick with his knife. He smiled when she came in — a big, comforting, understanding smile that brought a lump to her throat.

She sat down and whispered, 'I feel bad, Tom. Awfully bad. Poor Dad . . . '

Midnight whittled away, then said, encouragingly, 'Go ahead, gal. Don't mind me, just weep your heart out ef it'll do you any good.'

So she came and sat by him and wept for a few minutes, and then she felt a lot better because somehow she could feel the strength radiating from this big, dependable puncher and she knew he was her friend and to be trusted.

Midnight spoke at length, though seeming intent on his whittling. 'Gun De Leon's a professional gunnie.'

He got the girl's interest, as he expected he would.

'I don't understand?' she said.

'Wal,' he drawled, 'you hire professional gunmen. So the question is, who hired Gun De Leon to cause trouble with my late respected uncle — even to

51

the point of killin' him? You c'n bet it's something to do with this fence wire we're sellin', so I guess it's up to us to find out all we can about De Leon and the men back of him.'

'Us?' said the girl quickly. It did something to her heart, that one word. Us . . . there was a warming, companionable sound about it.

'Sure,' drawled the puncher; 'you'n me, gal. I reckon to put you on the pay-roll just as old Walt wanted it. It'll do you good to have some interest in life, instead of sittin' in a corner mopin'.'

She was fast recovering her spirits, and she stood up to the dominating cowboy. 'I don't mope,' she said. 'And if you call me 'gal' again there'll be trouble, you big roughneck. My name's Alexandra to my friends.'

Midnight whittled a hat on top of a head out of the stick and said, casually, 'Alexandra's too much to fit into any man's mouth. I guess you'll have to be Sandy . . . '

She looked over his shoulder at what he was making, then cried out in admiration. 'Why, it's me,' she exclaimed. 'That's the hat I wore when I rode in with you today. How clever!'

She went and sat against the open window to get the breeze that was coming with the approach of evening. Midnight rose slowly, went across, and picked her up, chair and all, and carried her to his seat behind the table.

'That's somethin' you must never do,' he said. 'Always sit an' face the door an' window in this office. Otherwise someone might get to thinkin' it's the new barbed-wire salesman sittin' there and take a shot at you.'

And then he said, with a quick grin, 'Besides, Sandy, I kinda like to feel you sittin' close to me. I reckon I ain't used to havin' a pretty gal so near me.'

They sat for an hour side by side at that table, talking earnestly, two young people who didn't know a thing about barbed-wire salesmanship but were determined to learn ... two young people planning how to put over a sales campaign in the face of a hostile Medina County. Then they went and ate a dreary meal of salt pork, beans and sweet potatoes in the even drearier dining-room at Palmers. Yet curiously neither seemed to notice the flavourless diet or the depressing surroundings.

★   ★   ★

Two days later they had a visitor. It was Ricketts, a cattleman who wanted to fence up his land. He was a veteran in the wars against Santa Anna and the Mexicans, and there wasn't much he feared from man nor beast. But he was also a cautious Texan business man.

He came bluntly to the point.

'What are you goin' to do about this fence war? It ain't no good buying wire from you, only to have it cut down at night by the fence busters.' He was an old man, yet full of vigour. He sat there with his long white moustaches drooping, yet his head was erect and there was a sparkle in his eyes as he talked fighting talk.

'The hell,' he swore, and then apologised to the lady present. 'I want to fence my land. I c'n buy a herd of pedigree Herefords from Colorado and raise more beef than bone, which I can't do with my scrub cattle. But I ain't buyin' no Herefords till I c'n fence in my land.'

Midnight said, 'So . . . why don't you fill in this hyar form and get the wire you want? It costs but a hundred and fifty to two hundred dollars a mile to fence in with barbs, cheaper'n any other form of fencin' and much more effective.'

The veteran looked at Midnight. He knew there was something back of the big fellar's mind.

'It'll cost much more than a coupla hundred dollars a mile if it's cut down the night after I erect it.'

Midnight leaned across the table, his

eyes calculating. 'Suppose I guarantee to maintain that fence for three months once it's up?'

The old man's eyes jerked wide open, then he said, 'You do that an' I'll sign an order for five thousand dollars worth of wire.' Sandy promptly came across with the order forms, but the old man held up his hand protestingly. 'Oh, no, not so fast. Before I sign I want to know how you're goin' to look after my fence for me.'

Midnight said, 'I've been waitin' for someone like you to come along. The way I see it, these fence busters dictate tactics. They've got the advantage of bein' the attackers, which makes 'em mighty toublesome. But ef they ran into more trouble than they bargained for, I guess they'd be a bit cooler afterwards. Maybe we might get to stickin' up wire without much interference while they got over their wounds.'

'Wounds?' asked Ricketts softly.

'You don't expect this fence business will settle itself without a lot more people gettin' hurt, do you? No, there's got to be trouble. Okay, then I want it the way I like it. I want to dictate the fightin'.'

'So?'

'So we'll put that wire up for you. It'll be done openly, just invitin' attack.'

'And when the attack come?'

'We'll be there to teach the fence busters a lesson.'

Ricketts sighed. 'We? Who's we, son? I ain't got many men, and after a day's ridin' they won't be able to patrol no fences for you.'

'We'll only call on 'em when the fightin' starts,' Tom said. 'Your fence will be patrolled for you.'

'By you an' your — er, pardner?' Old man Ricketts shot an amused glance at Sandy.

'Nope. I got friends, old-timer. Plenty friends. And I've already sent for 'em. Most are up in the new country, on the Staked Plains, an' it'll take a week or so for 'em to get here. But they'll get here, don't worry. Then there's three boys who were in Silverstone jail with me. Good boys. They only shot up a deputy — just for the fun of it. I guess the sher'f'll let 'em out when he gets my letter. Me an' the sher'f parted good friends. Besides, he didn't like that deputy none. They should be here in a day or two.'

'You figger you'll be able to pertect my wire?'

'Ef I don't — for three months — you don't have to pay me for it.'

Ricketts sighed. 'At the end of three months I guess I c'n look after it myself. Life should be easier back of a fence.'

Midnight dropped his feet to the floor. 'That means you'll sign?'

'It does.' Ricketts reached for the form and scrawled his name. Then he rose to go, spurs clinking as he moved. At the door he turned and said, 'I like you, son; I guess you've got spunk. But this is going to lead to a man-sized struggle all right — a bloody, lead-swoppin' battle, I reckon. Take care o' yourself, son, and the lady, too.'

The old man turned to go.

The door started to move, stuck as usual, then was booted open.

Ben Coe stood in the doorway, facing them.

5

He was red-faced and angry, and his eyes looked suspiciously from one to the other. Neither Sandy nor Midnight knew him, but the old man said, ironically, 'You comin' for wire, Ben?'

Ben Coe spat in disgust. 'Blasted wire,' he growled, at which the old man, with a parting nod to the young people, stepped past him and went out into the sunshine of Devine's main, fly-ridden street.

Midnight said courteously, politely, 'Howdy, stranger. Won't you take a chair?'

Ben Coe seemed curiously irresolute. And then he said, 'I don't talk with windows open,' and there was significance in his tone that wasn't lost on the sharp puncher.

Midnight just nodded and crossed to the door. Outside, squatting on his heels on the board sidewalk just under the window, was a scrub-faced puncher in faded jeans. He was rolling a cigarette as Midnight came up. Big Tom stood over him, legs astride, and said gently, 'Pardner, you're sure sittin' in the sun hyar. You should go sit in the shade of the Hayride — it's cooler, I reckon.'

The punch came lurching to his feet. He was pretty big, though a few inches short of Midnight's height. He snarled, 'The hell, cowboy, you own the sidewalk, too?'

Midnight's hands were hovering over his twin guns, his eyes narrow-slitted and hard as steel. He called sharply, 'Get back from that window, Sandy — right back!' And then he said, his voice grating, 'I don't like smells, pardner, an' sittin' right under that window you made one big smell into my office.'

The scrub-faced puncher went into a crouch, his right hand within inches of the single gun he carried. He snarled, 'I kill men fer less than that.'

Midnight said coldly, 'Go ahead, *killer*. Lets' see if you've guts enough to draw.'

But the man hadn't the guts, and suddenly he knew it and his flaming temper cooled instantly.

He said weakly, yet again, 'You don't own the sidewalk, do you? I wuz just restin'.'

Midnight said ironically, 'Sure, right where the sun's hottest.' He hadn't relaxed for one second; you don't, not with that kind of hombre ready to pull a gun the moment you're off guard. Big Tom's voice snapped, 'How long've you been there, stranger?'

'No more'n a few minutes,' grumbled the scrub-faced man, his eyes shifting uneasily. 'The hell, I'll go if you feel that way about it.'

He started to move away. Unexpectedly Midnight reached out a long arm and pulled off the man's faded, soiled hat. The next second it was pitched into the middle of the street, and Midnight's two guns were blazing in his hands as he pumped lead into the hat.

Eight rounds made it dance up and down in the dust, and then Midnight holstered his Colts. All he said was, 'Mighty good job your head wasn't inside that hat right then, pardner,' and then he came back into the office.

Sandy was looking white, and Midnight put his arm round her shoulders and said, 'You don't need to be afraid, Sandy. I guess I ain't got much to fear against hombres like that 'un out there.'

Sandy whispered, 'Tom, I'm worried. If that man was out there listening all the time that Mr. Ricketts was here — '

'Sure.' Midnight nodded. 'He'd know our plans, huh? Wal, I guess he was out there most of the time. I guess he heard, all right, and I guess he'll go back with his information to his pals. That kinda upsets our plans a bit, but we'll think about that later.'

The lines of worry were no less deep on Sandy's brow as she heard confirmation of her fears. 'Oh, Tom, we're up against a bad lot of men.'

'You're dead right we are, Sandy. But I guess them galoots is up against a bad lot o' man in me,' he grinned. 'I'm just a mean, mean man, as ready to shoot as look at a fellar.' He shoved his brown, laughing face closer. 'And didn't I show it? You think shootin' up that inoffensive hat was just a kid's trick. No, ma'am, it was not. It was just to let anyone who was interested know that I could use a gun. I guess the significance won't be overlooked.'

They turned to their visitor, suddenly remembering him. Midnight said, 'Guess I sure oughta thank you for wisin' me up to that fellar outside.' And then he waited for the man to introduce himself.

He did. He spoke harshly, 'I'm Ben Coe. The last time I came into this office someone got hurt. I guess it was the uncle you buried last week, Midnight.'

'You tellin' me you came hyar that day someone stuck up my uncle an' busted his skull for him?'

Coe rapped, 'I was — an' you c'n keep your hands off'n them guns, Midnight.' He came farther into the office; he was a brave man, Ben Coe. 'I came to warn off your uncle, came to tell him to get the hell outa town if he wanted to keep his hide whole. But De — ' He checked himself hastily. 'But someone else didn't figger things out like I did and took a bang at your relative. It was against my wishes to use violence, an' we had agreed to avoid it before we came here,' he ended shortly.

'So it was De Leon who bust open old Walt's head,' said Midnight softly. He hadn't missed that slight slip of Ben Coe's. 'Guess that's another score I've got to settle with the galoot.' Then he said abruptly, 'You didn't come here to tell me just that, Coe. What're you here for, pardner?'

Ben Coe went to the window and looked down on to the boardwalk. Satisfied, he came into the centre of the room again. He spoke bluntly. 'Midnight, I hate your guts, you an' all these people that sell fence wire and fix fences over the open range. I don't come here because I like you any, an' I guess ef I see a wire fence anywhere near my path I'll go across an' tear it down.'

Midnight inclined his head. 'That sure is straight talkin', pardner.'

Coe said, 'I believe in straight talkin' — an' straight dealin', too. An' what's happenin' around hyar ain't beginnin' to be as straight as I like it.'

Midnight tossed his makings across, and Ben Coe settled on a rickety chair and made a smoke. Midnight said, 'Just this once, Sandy gel, you c'n stand by the window and see no one comes an' listens to what we're sayin'. Keep well back outa sight, though. I reckon Mr. Coe is about to tell us somethin' mighty interestin'.'

Coe nodded shortly.

'Midnight, there's some mighty powerful people startin' in on this fence war. At first fence bustin' was done by fellars like me an' Jim Daly an' Oklahoma Smith. Men who saw their all goin' because someone stuck a fence across the best pastures and waterin'-places. We went and took most o' those fences down, I reckon, but people kept stickin' 'em up again, an' I see we can't go on fence bustin' for ever.'

His voice was weary; it was the voice of a dispirited, disillusioned man.

Then he went on, 'But some guys want this fence bustin' to go on. I reckon they're figgerin' on makin' a pile outa the shambles, some way. We didn't know it at first, but after a time we got to see that we were being used by these people for their own ends. They were employing paid agents to come around an' keep our hate smoulderin' — they were usin' us to terrorise cattlemen who wanted to fence in their land, and then they started to use us to beat up the men who came to the cattle country to sell the wire.'

'And it stuck in your gullet, being

used as a tool by these powerful people?' In a minute Midnight was going to ask who those people were.

Ben Coe exploded, 'It sure did. The hell, I ain't fightin' for Eastern capitalists, sitting on their fat backsides in Washington and New York. No, sir; if they want land they must come and get it themselves.'

'It's just dirty, fighting men with money. I thought you might get to know I brought in that party against your uncle a while back, and I wanted to keep the name of Coe clean, do you understand? I didn't want you to think I was ganged up with some sly, murderin' bunch of Eastern capitalists. I'll go on cuttin' your fences, Midnight, but you don't have to think I'm lyin' round a corner with a gun like that rattlesnake, De Leon.'

Midnight looked at him carefully and then came to an opinion. 'I believe you, Coe. I guess you are as you say — straight. Sorry there's this wire between us.' They could be good friends, these two.

Ben Coe grunted. 'Wire's a bad thing; no good'll come of it.'

Midnight said, 'That's how I figgered things, when I listened to prejudiced people who didn't know what they were talkin' about. Then I heard sounder arguments from a coupla people, an' now my mind's changed. I think wire's gonna be the makin' of Texas. I think it can bring prosperity even to you yet, Coe.'

Ben Coe snarled, 'Yeah? With no water and precious little grass and my stock dyin' like flies? I've been out for weeks now, keeping the herd together, then bustin' a fence an' drivin' em through so they could get their fill of water, then bein' driven back an' havin' to start all over again.'

'What do the Eastern financiers hope to get out of a range war over fencin'?'

Coe said, 'I don't rightly know. I'm guessin'. But I'll lay my guess agen any other man's.' He was restless and paced the flimsy little office as he went on,

'My guess is these Easterners don't give a hang who wins — fencers or fence busters. All they want to do is set one lot agen the other. They want the prairie to go up in flames, as it has done before in range wars. They want shootin' an' killin', an' a lot of rustlin' of stock.'

'Why?'

'Why? Because when there's range war two things become cheap — life . . . and land.'

Midnight nodded. 'I'm beginnin' to get it, Coe.'

'When there's war, land becomes dirt cheap. These Easterners know that Texas land is the finest cattle country in the world; they know its value will rise from year to year. And they want to buy up whole counties, as investments for their shareholders. Land prices are pretty high, right now, an' I guess they figger if they could have a range war, prices would drop an' they could step in an' buy accordingly.'

'Do you know them — or their agents?'

Coe shook his head. 'I don't reckon we'll ever know that. They're just people back in New York who send telegrams an' pay out money to trouble-makers. They've got a bunch here in Medina County. A nice pisenous bunch o' rattlesnakes. There's De Leon, Jud Brasswick, Ed Kanak an' one or two others.'

He paused, then said abruptly, 'Boss o' the lot is Stan Copey — the Longhorn. He's doin' most of the talkin' and building up for trouble. An' after what you did to him, Midnight, I reckon you sure made a bad enemy for yourself. I saw that fight. I also saw his fight with Will Addason. He picked on the old man deliberately an' beat the life outa him. Guess he'll do that to you ef he has chance — '

He stopped. Both turned. Sandy had come away from the window, her face ashen, her eyes big and brimming with tears. Big Tom Midnight understood and went across and stood by here. He explained, 'I should have told you before. This is Will Addason's daughter, Coe.'

Ben Coe's harsh face softened. He said contritely, 'I wouldn't have said anythin', ef I had known.'

Midnight reached up and let his long, strong fingers caress the girl's luxuriantly thick brown hair. He said, 'Miss Addason an' my uncle are the two people I mentioned who changed my mind about the value of fencing. I guess Miss Addason knows more about farmin' than a lot of us.'

She had got over her crying now, and was wiping away her tears with her back to them. She spoke and already her voice was firm and composed.

'You live in the Bottomland, Mr. Coe, I believe?' He said, 'Yes, down by Stag End.' She went on, 'We were on Bottomland, but in the Three Streams Valley from you. I guess it's much the same country, pretty bare and over-grazed. That's one of the reasons why my father wanted to wire the land. He swore it could be made into fine

72

farmland, but it would have to be grazed sensibly and given time to recover.'

'And what would you do for water, Miss Addason?' asked Coe gruffly.

She retorted, 'Dig for it. My father reckons that under the Bottomlands is so much water they'll never be able to get it all out. He was planning on fetching some windmills over from Tennessee when — when this happened. Why don't you try well-sinking, Mr. Coe? Then maybe you'll be wanting wire from us.'

Coe said, obstinately, 'It's too late, I guess. And I haven't the money to go digging holes all over the country until I strike water.'

He started to go. Then he said, 'You watch out, Midnight. You made a fool of the Longhorn a few days ago, an' he hates your guts for it. Don't kid yourself he'll always be easy as that to handle, 'cause he won't. He was tired after his first fight, an' pretty drunk, too.'

Midnight said, shortly, 'I never kid

myself. I knew he was pretty drunk or I wouldn't have fought the way I did. But thanks for the warning, Coe. As I said, we're on the wrong side of the fence to you. Maybe some day you'll get over and join us.'

Ben Coe said, 'Like hell I will!'

Then he went. When he had gone Sandy looked at a calendar that bore the name of a San Antonio seedsman and said, 'The Longhorn — he's the man that killed my father, isn't he? And now he's ganging up against us in this fence war.'

Big Tom Midnight hadn't returned to his seat. Instead he was standing right behind her, a slow smile on his face. He said, 'You're aimin' to kill the Longhorn yourself, ain't you, Sandy?' He wasn't shocked; it was what he expected of a woman on the frontier.

She wheeled in surprise. 'How do you know, Tom?'

He shrugged. 'Why else should you be totin' a gun down your shirt, Sandy?'

She said in exasperation, 'Can't I keep a thing from you, you big cow-puncher? How did you know, anyway?'

'Uncle Walt's twin-barrelled Derringer's missin', an' your figure's not improved much this last coupla days or so, Sandy. You figger out from there,' he grinned.

She stamped her foot in annoyance. 'Now you'll be talkin' me out of it, I suppose.' He noticed, as he had noticed before, that there were times when she lost her normal nice speech and talked homespun like himself. He also noticed that when she flushed, through anger, embarrassment or some similar emotion, she looked prettier than ever, and in consequence he was inclined to tease her into exasperation.

'Nope, Sandy, I won't be try'n to talk you out of anything. The only thing is, if I beat you to it, don't get sore at me. When hombres like the Longhorn tote guns it isn't time for arguin' as to who gets in the first shot agen him.' Then he added thoughtfully, 'That De Leon fellar — he's mine, though, Sandy, an' I don't want nobody to touch him till I catch up with the varmint.'

He started to adjust his belt and chaps and she knew he was going out. 'Where are you going?' she asked anxiously. She never liked being left alone in this cattleman's town.

He sighed. 'That fellar listenin' at the window kind of upsets plans, Sandy. Before, I intended the boys from Silverstone an' the Staked Plains should just hang around town till they were needed. Now that won't work, 'cause the fence busters'll be wise to any strangers hangin' around from now on.'

'So?'

'So I'm goin' out towards Silverstone, to camp on the trail until the boys come up. I reckon they'll have to lie up in the chaparall till they're needed.' Then he added, thoughtfully, 'I guess they're not gonna like that, lyin' out there in this heat, day after day.'

Sandy slipped on her packet.

'Where do you think you're goin'?' he rapped.

'The chaparall's no place for the boys,' she told him firmly. 'Besides I know a place where they can hide up fine and comfortable and be no more than an hour and half's ride out of town.'

He caught on quickly, and his grey-blue eyes warmed with enthusiasm. 'Your place in the Bottomlands, huh?' He snapped his fingers. 'Now, why didn't I think of that! Come on, Sandy; we'll go together. This office don't need us until the barbed wire's delivered, an' we c'n post off the order now, on our way out.'

He looked at the signature on the order form. In the Santa Anna war veteran's crude writing he read, 'Cal Ricketts.'

He said, 'Mr. Ricketts, you get my thanks for startin' us off in business.'

Sandy said, firmly, '*Our* thanks. I'm in this as much as you,' and though he raised his eyebrows he made no comment at the remark. Together they crossed to the livery stable for their horses.

Over in the Hayride Saloon a man who hadn't been drinking saw them canter past and promptly set down his full glass and took horse after them. He was a man with a scrub beard on his chin and evil in his heart for the man who had publicly humbled him.

6

The consignment of barbed wire for the Rickett order came to the San Antonio railhead, and was then brought by ox-drawn freighters into Devine town. Midnight rode out to meet it, and Sandy went with him.

When they saw the slow-moving cloud of dust far down the trail they knew it was the convoy and they turned into the shade of a clump of roadside cedars and sat down to await its approach.

At first it was quiet, the quiet of a vast wilderness, with only the occasional cry of some distant, winging game bird to disturb them. South and east of this tiny hill on which they rested stretched the great Coastal Prairie, with its fine black soil that had once been covered with tall grasses until erosion came to spoil it. West and north reared the tall mountains of the Sacramento Range and the vast flat highlands of the Edwards Plateau. Between lay a subtropical vegetation consisting mostly of mesquite and creosote bushes, chaparall and lechu-guilla-agave . . .

Sandy looked over the immense distances and said, 'Always when I see this view I say to myself, 'I never knew Texas was as big as this'.' Already she was getting over the shock of her father's death and could take an interest in things again.

Big Tom lay sprawled at her side, a piece of grass between his strong white teeth. He was watching the approach of the wagons with their straining oxen. He was also watching all approaches to the dusty trail because it seemed to him to be no bad place for a hold-up. He thought, 'If they've got sense they won't go cutting holes in the wire, they'll grab a-holt on it now an' destroy it before it can be used.' And he fell to wondering how you could destroy barbed wire, and

80

in the end gave it up, not being able to solve that problem.

When the wagons came near, their axles creaking an agonised protest, they rose and rode down to meet the teamsters. There were five wagons in the train, strong and heavy, with iron axles, and wheels nearly six feet high and bearing iron tyres six inches across. Twenty to thirty oxen drew them, and the largest freighters carried as much as seven thousand pounds.

Midnight said, as they approached the sweating beasts, 'At a cent a mile per hundred pounds, they sure make money out of this freighting.' And then they turned their horses, just ahead of the train, and headed the slow procession into the town of Devine.

The entire population turned out to see them come creaking through. They knew what was in those wagons, and some were hostile to the cargo. But while a few swore up at Midnight and shouted abuse at him, as well as threats, mostly the people watched in silence.

Midnight simply ignored the shouters, though he took a note of their faces, all the same.

Then the procession turned out of town and took the long, rutty lane towards the Ricketts' ranch. The old-timer, Ricketts, came down from the house veranda to meet them. He gave them greeting, then said, 'A coupla fellars just rode up from Devine to say that if I strung wire they'd string me. What's more, Midnight, I c'n tell you they meant it, too.'

Midnight and the girl looked down thoughtfully at him.

'What did you tell them?' asked Big Tom.

The old-timer's long-handled moustaches quivered. 'I didn't tell 'em nothin',' he said. 'I jes' pulled a gun on 'em an' snicked one o' the fellars' ears.' He chuckled. 'That's dandy shootin' fer an old man, eh, Midnight?' The incident seemed to have put him in rare fettle.

Midnight said, 'That means you're

goin' ahead with the fencin'?'

The wagons were pulling into the yard and there was such a noise of men shouting, whips cracking, oxen bellowing, and wagons creaking and groaning that Midnight had a hard time to hear the answer. But the gesture from the old man was unmistakable.

The fight was on.

They stayed while the wagons were unloaded of their heavy, spiky, flesh-tearing coils of wire, already reddening with rust. Then the oxen were bedded down for the night and the teamers had a barbecue supper before turning in.

Over a rough meal in the old man's kitchen, served by a Mexican houseboy, Ricketts said, 'It's time you were goin', Tom. You've got a good ride ahead of you; maybe you'd better start now.'

Big Tom rose and stretched. 'I'll be on hand tomorrow mornin' when your men start to fix the fences. It's a good week's work, but I don't reckon the fence busters'll wait to see it all up. My men'll be about the moment trouble starts.'

Sandy came out to the horse with him. She was troubled. 'You didn't tell the old man that the plan we made was overheard.'

Midnight swung into the creaking saddle and looked down at her. 'Nope,' he said decisively. 'I don't see why we should give him any worry. You heard what Ben Coe said? He said that the Eastern financiers are determined on a range war. Okay, let it start here on old Ricketts' ranch. I reckon the old boy won't be displeased none by a fight, anyway,' he added dryly.

Sandy looked up quickly and then down again, saying, 'And neither will you, Tom. I know you now.' She stretched up and patted his gloved hand. 'Be careful, Tom, if only for my sake. I — I don't want to be orphaned again so soon.'

She saw that tanned face, shadowed by the fading light, break into the big grin she loved, saw the flash of his teeth. And then he set her heart to pounding. He said, 'Honey, you don't need to worry at all. I'll come back — I'll always be comin' back for you, I reckon.'

Midnight rode to the Addason homestead over the Break-back Ridge, following a mule trail that the Indian traders had first made. It was rough going and rocky, and Midnight took it carefully, because he didn't want a blown horse so early in the night.

Finally he rode down the bare hillside that backed on to the distant Addason ranch. He was so near now that he sat easily in the saddle and sang softly a night-rider's lullaby to restless little dogies . . .

He stopped singing. Someone was moving parallel to him in the blackness of that moonless moment. Someone on a horse.

Then he heard a curse and a voice snarled, 'What'n hell have you to sing about, Jud?'

It was a voice he knew, but it took

Midnight a few moments to remember where he had last heard it. And then it came to him, and abruptly he reined in his horse.

For the voice was that of — the Longhorn.

The other horsemen moved across the face of the hillside, obliquely to the way he was going, and he heard the sound of creaking saddle leather grow fainter with each passing second. He also heard a growl from Jud, who said, 'The heck, it wasn't me singing,' but no one seemed concerned enough to pursue the matter further.

When they were beyond earshot, Midnight let out his breath with an exploding sigh. 'That was a near thing,' he muttered to himself, and then his brow puckered. It was too much of a coincidence that the fence busters should be out so near to the Addason homestead right after the delivery of the precious barbed wire.

Midnight thought, 'They've got to know the boys are here, in the Addason

86

place. They're gettin' into position across the mule trail to ambush us when we go back.' And he thought how lucky he had been to blunder into them like that — not only blunder in on them but also blunder safely away without being recognised. Perhaps because he had been singing he hadn't been suspected; sometimes it worked out that way.

Midnight didn't bother to argue with himself any more; instead he sent his horse hurrying down the slope until he saw the darker shape of the ranch-house. Then he sang again that plaintive little dirge about restless dogies, and so the man in the shadows knew him and let him approach.

It was Fred, one of the Callason brothers who had been in Silverstone jail with him. He was lazy and could think of a lot of reasons why he should ride away from work, but when there was the prospect of a fight or some excitement he perked up and was always there. Rob, his older brother, wasn't any different, either.

Fred said, softly, 'Hyar, Tom ... Hell, Tom, what'n Hades is the good of standin' guard here, night after night? Nothin' don't ever happen. Reckon we should fergit it an' climb into the hay, huh?' It was the plaint of a bored and weary cowboy.

Midnight said, 'Sure, climb into the hay, Fred — an' miss all the fun.' He could see the outline of the thin cowboy standing below, cuddling a rifle in the crook of his arm.

Fred said, quickly, 'Fun? Aw, now, Tom, I ain't missin' no fun, not after comin' all this way.' His voice was suddenly alive, his weariness miraculously dissipated by the news. 'When's it goin' to start?'

Midnight turned in the saddle and looked into the blackness in the direction of the old mule trail. He was doing some calculating.

'It c'n happen any time.' He kept his voice to a whisper. 'There's a passel o' fence-busters a-sittin' astride the old mule trail by now, I reckon. Guess they opine to open up on us as we ride past, only we won't ride past, now we know.'

Fred said, 'We goin' a-ridin', Tom?' — eagerly.

'Within an hour.' He pulled up the head of his champing horse and said, 'You might as well come in with me, Fred, an' get yourself ready. I don't reckon anyone'll be sneakin' up on us in the next hour or so.'

He touched spurs and the horse clattered into the yard and up to the rail before the farmhouse. Someone heard him and threw open the door to greet him, and a shaft of yellow oil-light fanned into the darkness. Midnight called quicky, 'Shut that door.' A man silhouetted against lamplight made a good target for a sniper in the hills with a rifle. He didn't think there'd be any shooting yet, but Midnight wasn't a man to take chances.

He went in quickly, while Fred hitched his horse for him and gave it water and a light feed and a rub down. All the boys were there, including some of old Will Addason's hands Standing just inside the door, smilingly acknowledging the greetings, Midnight peeled off his gloves and surveyed the scene.

The bunkhouse hadn't been big enough to take the extra men, so they were now living in the Addason house. There were blankets strewn untidily on the floor of the rough-timbered living-room, just as the punchers had climbed out of them that morning. The saddles they used for pillows had been pushed back against the log walls, and the place was a shambles of cigarette-butts, empty bottles, dirty coffee-pots, and articles of clothing and equipment strewn everywhere. Midnight thought, 'If Sandy could see her home now she'd sure get good an' mad!'

But Sandy wasn't there, and it was no good getting mad at cowboys who weren't used to anything better than a rough bunkhouse. They might be casual in their manners, but they had some good points, too. One was, they were loyal to him and were always ready to take his side in a fight.

A couple of the boys were already settling down for the night, but they got up again when they saw Midnight. Someone poured out a pot of strong coffee and hospitably shoved it into Midnight's hand. It was welcome after the long ride through the night. When he'd drunk, Midnight said, 'I guess things are goin' to happen, fellars — soon.' He looked at Addason's hands. He was doubtful of them.

Joe Culloch interpreted the glance and said, 'That's okay, Tom. These boys know what we're here for, and they're with us. They'd come a-gunnin', too, because of the way their old boss passed out, only I tell 'em someone's got to keep the ranch going.'

Midnight looked at the three Mexicans and decided they looked good boys; the negro he wasn't so sure about but he let it pass. He squatted against the wall by the log fire that Wee Jock

91

McCraw booted into a blaze and told them that the wire had arrived, it was to be erected the following morning, and he wanted his party to be on hand to give protection in case of a raid by the fence busters.

And then he told them how he had blundered into the Longhorn's party just back of the Addason ranch.

His brow puckered as he said, slowly, 'I just cain't figger how come they've tumbled to your bein' here, boys, but as sure as eggs break good an' easy, they do know. Right now I guess they're a-sittin' back there across the old mule trail, just waitin' for us to ride within gun range.'

Dour, sallow Max Jacinto, who got into fights because men in their drink spoke slightingly of the colour in his skin, gruntled, 'So we don' ride the mule trail, huh? We come aroun' and shoot 'em up from behind, huh?'

Midnight shook his head, and Mex's face fell with disappointment. 'Nope,' he said decisively. 'We got a job to do, an' that is to pertect the men fixin' up that wire I've sold old Ricketts. Okay, we don't go huntin' for trouble till that's done. Instead we walk our horses back up the face of the hill, keepin' east of the mule trail all the way, until we reach the cedar brake by the bush country. I reckon we'll have skirted any ambush by that time.'

The men growled and nodded, though it wasn't all approval. Skirting an ambush didn't seem fun. Beating up the ambushers sounded a whole lot better. Midnight heard and understood. His face cracked into a dry smile as he pulled on his gloves. 'Okay, boys, don't get too het up about it. We'll pass this ambush up — and fix a nice li'l ambush for the Longhorn ourselves. Yeah.?'

Wee Jock McCraw said, 'Now you're talkin', Tom. C'mon, let's go!'

In a moment every man was jubilantly grabbing for his kit and preparing for the ride ahead. While they were doing this one of the Mexicans, a young, lithe man of little more than twenty, came up and addressed Midnight, now standing with his back to the door.

'I'm comin' with your party, Tom. I'm Felipe, an' Miss Addason'll tell you I'm a good boy.'

Midnight looked into brown, shining eyes and considered Felipe looked to be more Indian than Mex and might be a good fighter, and he might need all the good fighters he could recruit. But he shook his head, all the same. 'I didn't tell Miss Addason I'd be takin' her boys. I guess you'd better stay here where you're most needed.'

Felipe's temper came up at that; like a lot of breeds, his passion was never far below the surface. He swore, 'Goldarn it, Tom, I ain't made to be farmer an' nurse to a lotta cows. Me, I'm a fighter, like my father — ' He checked himself when about to say something more, and then said, defiantly, 'The hell, I'm either comin' with you or I'm a-goin' to seek out the Longhorn an' join the fence busters.'

Midnight watched that savage brown young face keenly and thought, 'And you would, too, you Comanche!' It wasn't hard to guess what blood ran in Felipe's veins — the blood of the fierce Comanche Indians who would never make truce or parley with the invading white men from the east.

He said, 'Okay, Felipe, you c'n come,' but he thought that he would watch that boy closely, all the same.

When he saw that all the men had collected their belongings, he called, 'You, Cass, turn out the lamp.' He wasn't going to advertise their departure to the watchers in the hills by leaving in the full glare of the ranch-house light.

When they were ready he led his horse back up the hill, with the other, sweating, cursing punchers treading hard behind. It wasn't easy, climbing that bare shoulder of mountain, and it galled the men to have to do it while perfectly good horses trod on their heels. But Midnight knew that if the horses had to do that climb while carrying weight they'd be good for nothing once the mule trail on top was reached. And Midnight couldn't be certain that there mightn't be other ambushes all along the road back.

Over an hour later they reached level ground. They stopped for a breather for five minutes and then mounted and slowly cantered away. The moon stayed out most of the time, so the going was easy, and by three in the morning they were walking into the yard back of Ricketts' ranch. Ricketts and Sandy got up to greet them. Cal Ricketts looked at the men as they came crowding into the lighted main room, and his eyes were approving. These nine men looked tough; they'd put up a show that the fence busters wouldn't forget. With his own men, this was a force to be reckoned with.

Sandy had a smile for them, even at that early hour, and the men doffed their hats in respect as she came in. When she saw Felipe she looked surprised and exclaimed, 'What are you doing here, Felipe?'

Midnight was watching both closely. He felt that Sandy wasn't altogether pleased to see the man. But Felipe's lean Indian face broke into an easy smile and he simply said, 'I'm a buster of fence busters now, Miss Addason. Guess I couldn't stay on farmin' when I knew there was fightin' goin' on just over the hill.'

The men ate and joked and didn't seem to think at all, only Midnight who watched the eastern horizon and never forgot the plans he had made. When he saw the first glimmer of daylight over the eastern lowlands he rose, saying, 'Climb into them saddles, fellars. We've got to get into position to receive visitors, I guess, an' they mustn't see where we go.'

Outside the cold morning air struck into their bones and made them shiver. Sandy came out with them, though Midnight said, 'You go back, Sandy, gal. You don't need to catch cold out here.'

But she came out, all the same, and when he swung into the saddle she came and stood against his leg and spoke up softly to him.

He heard her whisper, 'Watch Felipe, Tom. He's wild and reckless and never gets out of trouble. He has a temper that's as savage as the Comanches' who were his ancestors . . . Watch what he does, Tom, else he'll sure bring trouble upon you.'

Midnight whispered back, 'I'll watch him, Sandy. I brought him because I figgered he'd be better with us than agen us.' And then he asked, 'What sort of trouble's the guy been in, Sandy?'

She considered for a moment and then said, 'Dad got an idea recently that he's gone back to scalping people.'

7

Midnight straightened and looked across at the rider with the tall, Mexican hat. He said, softly, 'Scalpin', huh? That's an Injun trick all right. What happened?'

'There were a couple of old settlers squatted down on the black soil of the Bottomland. One day a packman called and found they'd been killed — and scalped. Everyone put it down to an Indian raid, though the Indians are mostly up Wichita way now, and back beyond the Rio Grande, and nothing more was thought about it.'

'Then somehow Dad got to know that Felipe had once worked for the old pair, and he'd got wrong with them and been thrown out. And somehow Dad got the idea that Felipe might have done the scalping.'

Midnight said, 'Your dad might have been wrong.'

99

She shook her head. 'Dad didn't often make mistakes So . . . watch him, big man, watch him.' She patted his hand, and there was affection in the gesture. 'I'll be riding out this afternoon if everything's quiet; I've got a treat for you, but I'm not telling you what it is. I won't know where you're hid up, so you'll have to make a signal for me to see.'

Midnight said, 'I'll be watching for you, honey.'

They trotted off, just as light was suffusing over the chilly Texan landscape. They hadn't far to go. They went down the sunken trail a couple of miles, then set their horses into the scrub hills that rose tier upon tier behind the Ricketts' land.

When they were about to turn off to seek for a hiding-place that was good enough to accommodate their large party, Felipe came spurring up. Midnight didn't like the way he dug into his horse, nor the way he jerked back its head when he wanted it to stop. The beast was sweating and quivering with pain. Midnight thought, 'He's Indian, all right. Guess we might have a lot of trouble with this son of a gun.'

But Felipe was being friendly. He said, 'You follow me,' and the way he said it, so confidently, so sure that he would be obeyed, lifted Midnight's hackles a bit. 'Me,' Felipe boasted, 'I know this darn country well. I know every place to hide. Just back of that cedar break is a good place for us.'

It was as he said. Back of the cedars the land rose abruptly, forming almost a cliff, and back of it was a sudden fold in the ground that was big enough to take a party twice or three times their number, and so covered that even in the saddle they would be unseen from anywhere on the hills outside. There were some creosote bushes to provide shade against the rising, powerful sun, and sufficient grazing to last the horses most of the day.

Midnight rode into the place, looked at it and said, 'It'll do.' He felt that he didn't want to give praise to Felipe; somehow he resented the man and wished that he could find fault with this hide-out that he had shown them. But he couldn't, so he unsaddled and made himself comfortable.

Old Deaf Ector hadn't missed a thing. He put his blanket alongside Midnight and murmured, 'Guess you don't go fer that breed none, Tom,'

Midnight sat against his saddle and looked across to where Felipe was making a cover, using his blanket over some thorn branches as a shade against the sun. He said, softly, 'That guy makes my teeth edgy. I got a feelin' he spells trouble fer the outfit, buddy.'

Deaf Ector rolled a cigarette between stained, calloused fingers and looked across at Felipe. Ector had once been too near a gun when it went off, and the bang in his ear had done some damage which for a long time had made him deaf as a post, though now he didn't seem so bad. He was the oldest man in the party, a real old frontiersman and veteran of Sam Houston's army. When he spoke he said, gently, 'One false move outa that boy an' up comes my sights on him, Tom.'

And just as he spoke Felipe lifted his dark face and looked across. For a fraction of a second it seemed that his face lowered, and then the white of his teeth showed as he smiled at them before stretching luxuriantly in the shade from his colourful Mexican blanket.

Midnight lay down and looked at the sky through the lace-work of branches. He said, 'He saw us lookin' at him, Deaf. Knew we were talkin' about him. They're cute, them breeds; they seem to know as soon as a thought comes into your head.'

Ector didn't say anything, but Midnight knew he wasn't so deaf that he hadn't heard. Deaf Ector heard most things that were important to him. Midnight rolled over and fell asleep, his last thoughts being about the surprise that Sandy had promised — and about Sandy herself.

About noon he took a turn at watching himself. He climbed the short slope to a position which commanded a fine view not only of the whole valley in which the Ricketts' spread lay, but also, if he turned, of the rolling hill country that lifted behind him.

One man was all that was needed as a look-out, but early in the afternoon Wee Jock McCraw came swearing up on his stumpy legs, and then Rob Sallasan and Skippy Playfellow came and joined them for company.

Wee Jock looked down into the Ricketts' land, spat expertly at an unoffending black beetle, and said, 'That fence is sure comin' on apace, Tom. Reckon they'll be level with us any time now.'

Midnight looked again at the busy workers. They had come out with their wagons and teams the moment the sun was up, and all during the time he'd slept they'd been sweating away, driving in the pointed stakes and nailing up the malignant, flesh-tearing wire. Nearly two miles of wire had been erected that day so far, for old man Ricketts was down there himself and he'd put every man-jack on to the job. If there was to be a war with the fence busters, then old man Ricketts was aiming to provide a fence for them to war over.

But though there was this long tantalising fence shining in its newness under the fierce yellow sun, the fence busters didn't show their faces yet.

Midnight thought, 'Guess they'll be catchin' up on some sleep somewhere after sitting the cold night through alongside that mule trail.'

Hours ago they must have realised that they had been outwitted — maybe by now they might have remembered the singing cowboy who had ridden with them, and put two and two together. Maybe they would have ridden down to the Addason house and got the truth out of the boys. Midnight thought of that negro. He looked the kind to open his mouth easily if a gun pointed at his belly.

Well, the Longhorn would be sore, but that was only to be expected. They'd catch some sleep, and by now he guessed they'd be back somewhere out of sight over the shoulder of the hill. He also guessed they wouldn't be long before they struck. The fence busters didn't usually wait to see a fence completed before they came out with their cutters and the axes to smash up the stakes. Midnight thought, 'I guess it won't be long now.'

He also guessed the way the Longhorn would figure things, especially if that negro talked. All the time he had been at the Addason house Midnight had been careful to speak only of going to the Ricketts' place, never about hiding up some place beyond. So the Longhorn would figure that Midnight and his men were hiding up in the ranch-house, and maybe that was why the fence busters were letting this fence grow so far away from the ranch buildings.

Midnight watched the workers toiling, now directly below, and thought, 'The Longhorn's plans will be to swoop down an' chase off these workers, tear up as much wire as they can, then deal with us as we come a-peltin' from the Ricketts' ranch-house — where he thinks we are.' Only they weren't there. They'd thought ahead of the Longhorn, and were sitting cosily within half a mile of the wire, and with protective cover most of the way up to it.

When he felt he'd done long enough up there in the sun, Midnight left King Cass on the look-out and went gratefuly back to his patch of shade. Felipe was sharpening a wicked-looking bowie knife and didn't look up as he passed.

About an hour later they heard Cass calling down to them, and at once everybody rose and went running up the hill to his side. Midnight rapped, 'What is it, Cass?' as he threw himself face down by his follower's side.

King Cass, who sat a horse like the miner he mostly was, growled through his week-old beard, 'There's fellars sneakin' up on the wire workers. Lookit thar.'

Midnight followed the direction of the pointing finger. Through the scrub, parellel to the fence, the Longhorn was riding his men. They were in single file, walking their horses slowly and with caution, stopping now and then while their leaders made a reconnaisance over doubtful ground.

Midnight rapped, 'Get your horses ready. You, Jock, saddle mine for me, too.' Then he watched the scene below and calculated on his next move.

He counted the men as they appeared between some creosote bushes. He wasn't quite sure how many there were, but it seemed there were twelve or thireen — not as many as he had expected.

He found himself looking for Gun De Leon, trying to recognise him from the description men had given him, but he failed to identify him from that distance.

Down behind him he heard the clink

of bridle rings, and the heavy creak of saddle leather and knew that his party was ready to move out.

And then he saw something else. A movement along the sunken trail from the ranch-house. A solitary rider was loping easily along towards the fence workers. Even from that distance Midnight recognised the rider — it was Sandy, riding astride like a man.

With a sharp exclamation he half rose, anticipating what would happen. Then he paused and waited.

He heard Sandy's voice distantly as she called to the men working on the fence, and someone waved as if to indicate vaguely the scrub-infested hillside before them. He saw Sandy sit her horse for a minute as if looking for some sign from the brush that would guide her, and then she kicked her horse and turned its head up the slope.

And Midnight groaned, because she was heading straight for where the Longhorn's party was grouped in conclave back of a small cedar brake.

He slid down the slope, rising before he reached the bottom, and taking a flying leap off the steep hillside he landed into his saddle.

Wee Jock McCraw exclaimed, 'What the — ' as Midnight's flying body leapt over him.

Midnight rapped, holding in his plunging horse, 'That's bust up our plans, boys. Sandy's headin' this way — right bang into the arms of the Longhorn and his huskies. I'm going down on my own. You watch out from here an' come a-gunnin' if you see me in any trouble I can't get out of. But don't come unless you know you have to — *I don't want the Longhorn to know we're hid up here and not at the ranch-house.*'

Then he went galloping out through a tiny draw, and plunged into the bush. He rode quickly but cautiously. He wanted to get right up to the Longhorn's party before they spotted him. Surprise was always a considerable weapon in a fighter's armoury.

Once he came riding into the open over the top of a grassy hummock, and he was able to see Sandy again. She had drawn rein and was sitting her horse out there, while the Longhorn and his men pulled round her. Midnight halted and listened. He heard men's deep voices, then Sandy's, and hers sounded sharp and imperative, as though she were talking back at the men. Then again the men were speaking. Watching, Midnight saw one of the men reach suddenly out and grab Sandy's horse's bridle. Sandy tried to knock the hand away, but the movement set her horse rearing and she had enough on her mind to keep her saddle, much less start a fight with one of the Longhorn's huskies.

Midnight urged his horse into the scrub again, just as Sandy's voice floated up to him. He had to grin. It sounded as though Sandy was saying nasty things to the men around her.

The commotion drowned the sound of his approach. He was almost in among them when one of the men turned and shouted a warning. They all wheeled their horses to face him, their hands going for their guns. Then they saw they were faced by one man and he was without weapons in his hands, so no one drew, confident in their superior numbers.

Midnight rode coolly right in among them, saying, 'Let go that girl's hoss, fellar.'

The man let go immediately. Midnight had a way of giving an order that made men instantly obey. Midnight shoved his horse between Sandy and the men. She smiled at him, but he wasn't looking her way this time. He heard her say, softly, 'Good boy, Tom. I knew you'd come an' get me.'

The Longhorn got over his surprise and brought his horse wheeling round. Midnight looked into that big, swarthy face, with the sun-narrowed slits of eyes, the blue scrub chin and the matted hair that made him look like the Texas longhorn he was named after.

And Midnight didn't like him one bit.

The Longhorn snarled, 'You . . . blast you! Where'n Hades did you spring from?' His men were formed into a threatening crescent on either side of him, facing the man and the girl.

Midnight said, 'That's no concern of your'n, Longhorn.' And then he heard the girl behind him gasp, and involuntarily his head swung round.

Sandy called. 'Longhorn? You're Longhorn, who killed my father?'

Longhorn's heavy, bull-like head jerked up at that. But he didn't say anything, though it wasn't for fear or shame or any similar emotion. There was a sneer on his thick, drooping lips, and perhaps it was that that stung . . .

Astonished, Midnight suddenly heard the girl shout, 'Go for your gun, Longhorn! I'm gonna kill you like you killed my father!'

Midnight's head whipped round again. He saw Sandy diving into her shirt front to get the Derringer.

'You darned fool, Sandy,' he roared,

and knocked her out of the saddle. In the same movement his heels kicked into his horse and sent it careering in among the Longhorn's men. There was turmoil as the beast reared and lashed out, then Midnight had it under control again.

And the Longhorn, guns just clearing the leathers, found a cold hard barrel ramming into his stomach.

Midnight stood in his stirrups and shouted, 'Get back, the hull lot o' you. An' keep goin', or I'll blow the Longhorn's stomach through his back.'

The Longhorn could only sit and snarl his hatred, while his men retired a dozen yards. They sat their horses stiffly, ready to reach for gun-holsters the second they saw an opening, but Midnight wasn't giving any.

He called, 'I'm lookin' for a low-down gunman who shoots at unarmed men from around corners. His name's De Leon. Which one of you's De Leon?'

Nobody moved. Midnight jeered, 'Scared,

huh? Not so brave suddenly, eh? Come on, De Leon, let's see your face'

The Longhorn snarled, 'He ain't with us. What're you gonna do with me?'

Midnight didn't know whether to believe him, but when no one came forward to announce himself as Gun De Leon he was forced to believe that the Longhorn might be speaking the truth.

So he sighed and relaxed and said, 'Okay, if he's not here to hear me, when next you see him tell him he ain't got long to live.'

Then he jabbed the gun even harder into the Longhorn's stomach, so that a gasp came from him, and he said, 'Keep ridin', you critters. Keep ridin' right out of this part of the country, an' if I see you back here, so help me I'll blow your heads off.'

One of them called, 'What about the Longhorn? We don't go without him.'

They sat there, not moving. Midnight hesitated, then said, 'Okay, I'll send him after you unharmed, when you get out of pistol range.'

Still they hesitated, threatening and sullen on their restless, curvetting horses. But the Longhorn settled the matter for them. His voice came out harshly. 'Do as he says. I guess he'll keep his word. If he don't, come back an' perforate him.'

The men turned and walked their horses away at that, and when they were a good hundred yards down the trail Midnight said, curtly, 'Okay, brother, you c'n follow now. But remember what I said — keep off this range if you want to keep a watertight skin.'

The Longhorn rode his horse about a dozen yards, and then pulled his head round. His face was a picture of sullen hatred and menace, and his voice was as rough as the gravel on a hill track.

'You think you're good, Midnight.' He spat his own opinion into the dust. 'You think you've bested us because of this li'l shindig. But don't kid yourself,

116

cowboy; we ain't started in on you yet. You don't know it but you're bucking one of the biggest things that ever hit Texas.'

Midnight said, quietly, 'Sure — money from the East, an' plenty of it. So what? I never saw a dollar kill a man as fast as King Colt here.'

The Longhorn spat again. 'You'll find so many guns agen you, you'll never even hear your own. There's trouble comin', Midnight, big trouble. Only it ain't no good your tryin' to pull out now — you've left it too late, I reckon.' He leaned forward in his saddle, the better to display his vindictiveness. 'You laid hands on me, cowboy, an' I don't forgive that!'

Midnight for answer contemptuously shoved his guns back into their holsters. It didn't induce the Longhorn to reach for his own. He knew those guns could come out again fast enough, and the one demonstration of a lightning draw had been sufficient for his sense of caution. Instead he rasped, 'The war's just starting, cowboy. You see ef I ain't right!'

Then he savaged the sides of his mare with sharp-pointed Mexican rowels and stormed off after his allies. Midnight watched till he was safely out of range, then turned to Sandy.

An exclamation of concern broke from him. She was still lying where he had knocked her, and her face was white now with pain.

He looked again after the Longhorn and his party and then vaulted quickly out of the saddle and lifted the girl's head. She tried to smile through her pain, and said, 'You hit awfully hard, Tom. Guess you an' the floor just about knocked me out. But I'll be better in a moment.'

Big Tom Midnight lifted her gently and slowly carried her to her horse. His face was contrite and yet there was that determined, obstinate streak in his expression.

'I'm sorry, you know I'm sorry, honey. I just had to do it. You can't get a gun out from a shirt in time to shoot down a gun-totin' huckster like the Longhorn. If I hadn't interfered they'd all have started shootin', an' then where would you have been?'

She struggled upright in his arms and sighed, 'I guess you're right, Tom. But you know how I feel about the fellar.'

'Sure, I know, honey.' He swung her into the saddle and patted her arm consolingly. A glance after the Longhorn showed him and his party steadily trotting away along a hill trail southwards. 'But you should leave killin' a man to me. I'll get him for you one day, I promise.'

He swung into the saddle and sat there, watching the Longhorn party of fence busters until they were safely out of sight. He guessed that after his intervention they woudn't go down now and attack the working party along the fence line. That would come another day.

The girl said, 'Why did you let him go when you had him covered?'

Midnight looked surprised. 'Sure, now,' he exclaimed, 'didn't you hear me promise to let him go if they rode off an' left us alone? I couldn't break my word to a varmint like that, could I?'

Sandy said, meekly, 'I guess not, Tom. You're right, of course; I guess you always seem to be right.'

Then Midnight smiled and asked two questions. 'You all right now, Sandy gal? An' what's in them saddle-bags — the surprise?'

She smiled back and straightened her hair. The colour had returned to her cheeks, and she seemed well enough again. She nodded, 'It's the surprise, all right. Guess what? I found some flour yesterday, so I baked some white bread. I reckon you an' the boys'll enjoy that after corn bread.'

Midnight slapped his thigh. 'White bread! Now that sure sounds nice an' tasty. Come on up an' share it with the boys.'

He turned and together they rode into the knee-high scrub and into the clumps of black jack and post oak. After they had been riding for some time Sandy sighed and said, 'I hate to have to tell you, Tom, but trouble's already started thick an' plenty for you.'

Midnight reined in surprise, and shoved his broad-brimmed hat to the back of his head, the better to see her. 'What's on your mind,' he asked softly. 'Anythin' happened while I've been away?'

He saw there were tears brimming to her eyes, tears of vexation and disappointment. 'Oh, Tom, they're dirty fighters! They've bought the law an' turned it agen us. The sheriff's been along to say that if you bring any more wire into the county, it'll be impounded and you'll get slapped into jail. Oh, Tom, just when I thought we were going to get started in business!'

8

The wail in her voice seemed to carry for seconds afterwards, drifting like an October mist among the chaparall. He stared at her, digesting the information, and then she heard his voice, and it was just as cool, just as humorous, just as slow-drawling as ever.

'Sure, now,' he said, 'they must be mighty worried about us to go so far . . . ' He was patting her hand again consolingly. Nothing seemed to get this man ruffled and down, and his strength and confidence checked the tears that were near to falling.

She looked through a blur of unshed tears and said, 'Oh, Tom, it's wonderful the way you never let up. No wonder your uncle wanted you for this job.'

They turned and rode up the hill together, Midnight still holding her hand. He said, 'Tell me more about what the sheriff said.'

She shook her head. 'I think I've told you everything, Tom. That's all he said — and he didn't sound pleasant about it, either. Just that I had to tell you there was a ban from now on in regard to the import of wire, barbed or plain, into Medina County, and that anyone fetching it in would have it impounded under a sheriff's order and the persons responsible clapped into jail.'

Midnight took the lead into the narrow draw that led to their hiding-place. His voice trailed back, 'Jails somehow don't frighten me. I guess I've spent too much time in 'em to worry. I reckon I've never yet been in a jail I couldn't have bust out of in maybe a coupla hours at most.'

She called, 'But what are you going to do, Tom?'

'Do?' he repeated. 'I guess we won't do a darned thing until that fence is up an' we're sure it's gonna stay up. Then I'll go into town an' talk with the sher'f, I guess.'

He dismounted, then reached up and pulled her gently from the saddle. 'And you're to quit worrying, honey,' he said severely. 'Goddam it, you don't think a sher'f's gonna upset our li'l business, do you?'

She looked up at him, saw the breadth of his shoulders, the muscle on his bare forearms, the strength in that fine young face, and suddenly she broke into a smile and said, softly, 'I guess there's no need to worry with you around, Tom.'

Coffee — that inevitable accompaniment of any Texan's meal — soon came up, and then they sat in a circle, Sandy in the shade of Felipe's gaudy Mexican blanket, and talked.

Midnight told his men what had happened in his encounter with the Longhorn and his party, and then gave the news that the sheriff was outlawing the import of fence material.

He sat with a hunk of soft white bread in his hand and spoke in that slow, drawling voice. 'I guess I cain't quite figger out things. Little more than a week or two ago I was dead agen the men that put wire across the open range, yet now I find myself leading in the battle to get it fixed pronto.'

The men watched him while they ate the unusual white bread, so delicate and tasty after their normal unleavened corn loaf. Mostly they didn't give a hang what they were fighting for; Midnight, their old friend of many a battle, had said he needed help, so here they were all ready to stand by him. They weren't professional gun-toters, but there was only a hairline of distinction between them and the breed.

Sandy said, 'Maybe you've learned a few things since sitting in that office.'

Midnight nodded slowly. 'I guess that's it. I guess maybe now I c'n see there's a whole lot to be said for controlling the range, an' not eatin' the heart out of it as we're mostly doin'. Yeah, looks like I'm a whole-hoggin' fence man, an' prepared to fight for what I believe in.'

Wee dwarfish Jock McCraw growled from his coffee, 'I guess you got a fight comin' at that, Tom, what with the Longhorn an' now the sher'f movin' in agen you. But I'd keep my eyes skinned for the Longhorn, mostly. What we heard o' that fellar even far back on the Staked Plains wasn't good.' He spat in disgust. 'From what's said of him, he's jes' undiluted rattler pisen.'

Old Deaf Ector spoke. He got around to thinking while most other people were opening their mouths and saying nothing. 'What I cain't figger,' he said, 'is why the sher'f's movin in on this matter.'

King Cass answered. 'Maybe because someone's paid him to make this move. Sher'f Con Tierney don't amount to much, an' I reckon he could be bought.'

'By the blamed Eastern financiers?'

'I cain't think of no other people right now.'

'But that don't answer the question,' Deaf Ector persisted. 'Why has the galoot put this ban on the wire? It's kinda contrary, see? Wire's the stuff that'll set the range afire an' give the Easterners a range war. What's their object, then, in stoppin' the import of the wire? How d'you figger that out?'

Midnight shrugged. 'Right now I don't. But there's one thing I'm sure on, an' that's that these same Easterners are back of this move with their bags full o' Yankee dollars. Maybe it looks contradictory; all the same, you bet it adds up to them in the final count.' He rose, suddenly impatient with talk. 'Anyway, you bet we'll know who's back of it, all in good time, fellars.'

With that he dismissed the subject. Talking didn't get them any nearer solving the mystery; meantime there were more important matters to go into.

He gave orders. 'We're ridin' that fence every night from now on. Until it's built it's gonna be our responsibility to see that no one comes a-bustin' in.

Old man Ricketts' men can't work at that pace all day an' guard the fence at night, but once it's up, I reckon they can do their share of fence ridin'.'

Mex Jacinto was looking to the breech of his Colt. He growled, 'You think they'll come?'

'What do you think?' Midnight's grim tone gave his own answer.

Jacinto clicked back the breech and carefully holstered his gun. Back came his growl, 'I think it cain't come quick enough.'

Then Midnight mounted to ride with Sandy back to the ranch. He was going to arrange for a couple of pack mules to be brought up after dark with food, extra blankets and ammunition. He guessed they would be camping out for quite a few days now.

Ricketts was back at the ranch-house, having come along ahead of his men. When he heard what had happened he wanted to bring Midnight's men in. 'The Longhorn knows they're round about; if what you say is right about that blabbin' negro, he'll even know how many men you've got. What's the sense in keepin' 'em out there?'

Midnight shrugged. 'I guess it's just the way I wouldn't want it to happen, if I were in the Longhorn's boots. Ef they come in to the ranch he'll soon know it, an' he'll know where to expect trouble when it comes. All right, while we hide in the hills he won't know where to expect us, an' that gives us the advantage of surprise. I reckon we'll need all the help we c'n get,' he added grimly.

'You think they'll come in greater force?' asked the old man, and Midnight's answer was the same question that he had put to Mex Jacinto.

'What do you think?'

The old man nodded and sucked on a corn cob that had been made years ago half-way across a continent. He was trying to figure out a few things that were puzzling him.

'You oughta go quickly an' see that sher'f,' he said abruptly.

Midnight looked at him. 'You know the sher'f? What kinda man is he?'

'Con Tierney? Oh, he's not much of a fellar. I guess he took to sheriffin' 'cause that's a mite easier'n raisin' beef. And he's always been one to take whatever you had in your hand,' he added significantly.

'Like that, eh?' Midnight looked out at the gathering dusk. 'These Easterners sure got plenty to hold out to him, too, an' he won't be the first sher'f to be bought, I guess.'

Then Sandy said, 'Tom, I can't see what good can come by bribing the sheriff to stop our wire imports. It just doesn't make sense.'

But Midnight smiled and said, 'It does, honey, only we don't quite see it straight yet.' Then his manner changed. 'The heck,' he said. 'Did you hear me call you honey? Now, how long've I been doin' that, uh?'

Sandy said demurely. 'Quite a long time.'

'Then,' said Tom firmly, 'you jes' tick

me off when you hear me again. For land's sake, if anyone hears me they'll sure think I'm a-sparking you.'

'And you're not?' The girl faced him provocatively, her eyes dancing. The old man watched, saw the flush to her face and noticed the little catch in her voice as she spoke, and he smiled to himself. Many times he had watched this same thing happen on the prairie . . .

She didn't know whether Midnight was serious or bantering, for his face looked as stern as ever as he exclaimed, 'Lord, Sandy, what're you sayin'! What would I be doin', sparkin' you, an' me your adopted daddy?'

She knew he was teasing her and she threw back her head and laughed. 'Go right on callin' me honey, Tom — I like it.' Then she was away into the kitchen to see that the saddlebags were well filled for when Midnight took the pack ponies out later.

It was two nights later that the fence busters struck and — Midnight saw the key to several minor mysteries.

As soon as dusk came, Midnight would ride down from the foothills with his men and post them along the curving wire fence. At first, when the fence was not overlong and the moon rode high, the men dismounted and settled down to keep watch along their particular stretch of wire; but as the fence lengthened it meant that a constant patrol had to be maintained in order to provide complete coverage over the work.

This night, right at the end of the wire, Rob Callasan had turned and was riding to meet his brother, when suddenly he heard sounds ahead and caught the clink of metal as it gripped and cut into wire.

He moved forward cautiously, in order to see what was happening. The moon was little more than a quarter full, so there was not over much light. He came close up to the fence busters, and saw what they were doing, then raised the alarm.

There were a lot of them, working

there; it was too dark for a count, but he had a feeling there could have been several dozen fence busters tearing into that fence. That meant their own force was well out-numbered, added to which they were strung out over a distance of several miles.

He struck a match and held it to his face as if to light a cigarette. 'Doggone it,' someone whispered in exasperated tones, 'what son of a she-mule's lightin' a cigarette? *Put that light out, you blamed idiot!*'

Rob acted the part well. At once he doused the light, and growled something in the darkness which contained the words ' . . . kinda forgot.' And that seemed to satisfy them.

Then he dismounted, and stood almost on top of them, while they worked with frantic haste. Men with cutters were chopping up the precious barbed wire into useless lengths all along about a quarter of a mile of fence — and there is quite a lot of wire in a quarter of a mile of cattle fencing.

Others were dragging up the fence posts and building them into a pile. Rob caught the whiff of kerosene and knew they were being soaked preparatory to being set on fire.

He drew out his gun and waited to shoot down any man who went to light the pyre. These line posts were nearly as valuable as barbed wire in this part of the country, and it would take some time to replace them. Losing the barbed wire was quite bad enough without the further loss of posts.

About five minutes later a coyote raised a howl, coughed in the middle of it, then tried again. Rob got back on his horse and tied a clean white cloth around his neck. He guessed that back there up the line several of the boys, including his brother, would be doing the same.

At that moment a hoarse voice rasped, 'Guess that'll be enough, fellars. Touch off that pile an' let's get the hell outa here afore any fence riders come up.'

134

A match flared in the darkness. Rob promptly loosed off and shattered the arm that held the match. Across the pile two more guns barked. The man deputed to light that fire went stamping hoarsely around as three heavy .45 bullets hit him almost simultaneously.

There was pandemonium at that. Guns flamed as the fence busters shot back at where the Colts had spoken. Then the Colts spoke again, only this time there were five of them, all pouring bullets into the mass of fleeing fence busters.

'Get to your hosses,' roared a voice, and in the distance Midnight, walking slowly away from the battle, heard it and recognised it for the Longhorn's.

A few seconds later the confusion became greater as a cry went up, 'The hosses have gone. Someone's taken them . . . '

In a moment their superior numbers were considerably discounted. All down the fence and from the ranch itself men were riding like fury to join Midnight's handful of guards. And high over the din they heard a blood-curdling whoop that could have been the war-cry of some lusting Comanche.

The the bull voice of the Longhorn shouted commands. 'Get together. Keep going back into the scrub. They can't follow there in the dark on hosses.'

It should have been a glorious victory for the fence busters, instead of which it was a rout. That pile of fence poles was to have flamed and brought the fence riders one by one into a trap formed by the Longhorn's mounted men: only the trap had been sprung prematurely, and now they were on foot and opposed by a growing band of resolute fighters.

Riding steadily away with the fence busters' horses, Midnight, Wee Jock McCraw and Joe Culloch heard the sounds of battle going back up the scrub slopes, and grew impatient to be in the thick of it. When they had ridden half a mile, therefore, Midnight gave the word to set the horses loose, and then all turned and galloped back to where the red stabs of flame marked the fighting.

Wee Jock shouted as they galloped together, 'By God, Tom, things couldn't have worked better, could they?'

And Midnight nodded in the darkness, a very satisfied nod. Everything had gone to plan. First the signal — a cigarette being lighted when it had been arranged that no one should smoke the night through. And then the pause to give the nearest fence riders chance to scout around in the darkness, find the fence busters' horses, deal with the couple of men watching over them, and then drive them quietly away.

Now the plan was to give the fence busters such a lesson that they wouldn't be in a hurry to come back for more fighting.

As they galloped up, Midnight and his men saw shadows loom up out of the darkness — other mounted men. Their guns were out and pointing, and then they saw that, like themselves, these other riders were wearing white cloths around their necks. It was the identification mark of Midnight's men.

It proved very useful, that white cloth that was worn by Midnight's party. They never had to waste a shot, but there was many a fence buster winged by his own supporters in mistake for a Midnight man.

The fight continued for about an hour, and then it petered off. Some of the fence busters probably found their wandering horses and mounted and rode off, while the rest — those that could walk — clambered painfully through the dark thorn scrub on the long trail across country to the town to Devine from which they had set out.

But there were several who lay out on that hillside who would never walk again. And one was old Deaf Ector, who had fought his last battle, and the other was a fence buster who had died in a manner that white men abhorred.

9

Dawn found them riding slowly, wearily, into the corral back of the Ricketts' ranch. They would have felt jubilant over their victory, but for the fact that old Deaf Ector was being brought in on a wagon.

A few of the men had received wounds. King Cass had lost a finger, but he made light of it, saying roughly, he had plenty left, hadn't he? And Fred Callason and Skippy Playfellow both needed bandages for their heads.

'Yeah,' said the old rancher, looking grimly at them as they came in for breakfast. 'But you were lucky, all the same. Ef that plan hadn't worked so sweetly, I guess I'd be diggin' a hull lot o' holes this mornin'.'

He stood looking up at Midnight, who hadn't dismounted. 'You goin' some place, Tom?'

Midnight nodded. He didn't show the fatigue as his men did. 'I'm a-goin' to visit a stinkin' polecat without delay,' he said, and then Sandy came out with hot coffee to fortify him for his early morning ride.

'The sher'f, huh?' Old Ricketts' eyes narrowed. 'Reckon you're takin' an all-fired risk, ridin' into Devine town this mornin', Tom. Maybe some o' the boys had better go with you.'

Midnight handed the mug back to Sandy. 'I got to doin' a bit of thinkin' in the dark of last night,' he said slowly. 'Maybe I've begun to see what's back o' this move to bring in the law agen us. So . . . I'm goin' to try'n spike their guns, goldarn 'em.'

★   ★   ★

Tierney wasn't expecting Midnight. He was behind his desk, feet up, a hat over his face, indulging in an early morning siesta because he had been up late the previous night and felt tired.

140

Sheriff Con Tierney was a man who very soon felt tired, and that was why he had run for sheriff and made sure of getting the job. If you were sheriff, even of a small town like Devine, there were quite good pickings to be had if you weren't scrupulous. Con Tierney wasn't.

Midnight leisurely removed his gloves, then drew up a chair and sat down with his feet comfortably on the desk He waited patiently for the sheriff to waken and see him, and he didn't have long to wait.

Tierney must have sensed that someone had come into his office, and after a reluctant hesitation his hand came up and pushed back his hat so that his bleary eyes could see out from under it. He didn't look so good that morning, and he wasn't feeling good, either. When he saw who his visitor was, he didn't feel any better.

His feet thudded to the floor, and his hat fell off. His eyes widened with apprehension and he half rose to his feet.

'Midnight!' he exclaimed. 'What do you want hyar, fence pedlar?'

Midnight spoke gently. 'Fence pedlar? You wouldn't be just a mite offensive with that label, would you, sher'f?'

The sheriff's eyes flickered to the well-worn butts of Midnight's guns, saw that the lazy-looking cowboy's hands weren't over far from them, and retracted hastily.

'Nope — no offence meant at all, Midnight. Guess I was just startled at seein' you, that's all.'

Midnight nodded agreeably. 'I'll let it pass, then . . . An' now you can startle me by tellin' me what you told Miss Addason out at the Ricketts' spread earlier this week.'

'Okay, I'll tell you. You're a stranger to Devine, an' we don't like strangers.' A murmur of approval rose from the crowd outside. Tierney went on, 'Ever since you came here, you've been the centre of trouble an' disturbance, and as sheriff I ain't standin' for any more.'

Midnight said, bluntly, 'What trouble

an' what disturbance?' He had his back to the crowd, but he could feel that they were coming slowly, threateningly closer.

The sheriff swallowed. 'You had a fight the first day here!'

Midnight said, 'So what? The Longhorn had two fights that day, I 'member. An' in the first he killed his opponent, but you don't seem to have done anythin' about that, sher'f.'

Tierney said, harshly, 'It was a fair fist fight, an' just too bad the old man's ticker didn't survive it. What happens after fair fights don't concern the law in Texas, an' you know it.'

'Go on, then. Let's know more of the trouble I've caused.'

'You've said publicly you're out to shoot Gun De Leon for killin' your uncle. We don't allow vendettas in Devine.'

'You allow killers to get away with their crimes, though?'

Tierney bristled. 'Gun De Leon's got to hell outa the county, so far as I know.

If he shows up, I guess I'll do somep'n about it.' Then he played some high cards. 'You're a disturber of the peace, Midnight, and you're getting the citizens' backs up agen you.'

Midnight thought, 'So my guess was good . . .'

Tierney went on with his bluster. 'We know you're out to steam-roller wire sales on to the community, and we know you've imported gunmen from as far away as the Staked Plains to help you. You're bein' warned, Midnight; we don't stand for hoodlums in Devine. The slightest trouble from you and I'll raise a posse and hunt you down, you and every last friend of yours.'

Then Midnight drawled, 'An' every last friend of mine. I guess, would be anyone who did trade with me for wire, huh? And by a coincidence your posse would jes' nacherly consist of all them people who call for open range an' no fencin'?' He grunted. 'Uh, uh, Tierney, you ain't so clever as I thought. It's

144

stickin' out a mile now, what's happened.'

Tierney came lumbering to his feet, his face heavy with threat. 'By God, Midnight, I don't like your tone. Remember, I'm sheriff of this township, an' if you don't keep a civil tongue I'll clap you behind bars, you see ef I don't.'

Midnight came to his feet. He took longer than the sheriff, but then he was a much taller man. And when he was upright he stretched and yawned in the sheriff's face.

'Guess I'm tired, sher'f. Bein' up all night kinda keeps you weary the next day — *don't it?*' The question shot out so suddenly that the sheriff was startled and for a few seconds yammered without saying anything coherent.

So Midnight put on his gloves and made his remark plainer. 'You weren't by any chance out with them blamed fence busters last night to see fair play, were you, Tierney?'

The sheriff started, because the shot

was near to the mark, and once again he had to resort to bluster.

'The hell, I've had enough of you, you goldarn trouble-shooter. Get out of this office, and remember, *I'm laying fer you an' your friends. Make one false move an' I'm comin' after you with all the guns I can muster.*'

Midnight nodded easily. 'That's exactly what I came here to learn,' he smiled. 'Though I'd made a guess that's how things stood way back about two last night in the bright moonlight.'

The sheriff said, 'The hell, there wasn't much moon — ' then stopped, seeing the trap he had fallen into.

'So you were out?' said Midnight softly. 'It's good to know who you're fighting.'

They stood in the doorway. For the first time Midnight bothered to look at the crowd. The road outside the sheriff's office was solid with the male citizenry of Devine. They were so hostile that Midnight almost thought he could hear their malignant thoughts buzzing past his head. He stepped out on to the covered sidewalk as though he were alone in the street.

The sheriff followed him. He was a fool; he had to try and show his authority before his audience.

'You've had your warnin', Midnight. Send your gunnies home an' don't try'n import any more wire into Devine area, get me?'

'I get you.' Midnight nodded absently. He was calculating his chances on reaching his horse through this throng. A lot of the men looked as though they had just come out of a war, and these were to the front and particularly threatening.

He turned casually. 'That means when my present stocks run out I don't get no more?' The sheriff nodded, and there was a triumphant gleam in his eyes. 'It's a good job I've got pretty good stocks, then, ain't it?' said Midnight cheerfully. 'Guess I can hold out until the Texas Senate hears about this an' does somep'n.'

Tierney snarled, 'It'll take 'em years

to make their minds up.' Then, suspiciously, 'What's this about stocks? I didn't know you got stocks. Where'd you keep 'em.'

Midnight truthfully answered, 'Out at the Ricketts' spread, of course.'

Then he walked straight towards the crowd.

Not a man moved to let him by. He stopped when he could move no farther. A man with eyes that were bloodshot from lack of sleep said, 'We want you, you critter, fer what you done last night.'

Midnight went back two quick paces, then stood facing them, hands held slightly away from his body in readiness for a lightning draw.

He called clearly, 'Who wants me c'n come an' get me.'

Still not a man moved. Each waited for his neighbour to start the duel, each was reluctant to begin it himself. Those guns of Midnight's had a fine, professional polish to their handles, and the face that confronted them was the face of a man prepared to shoot his way out of this threatening situation . . . particularly they didn't like the look in those level, grey-blue eyes, the eyes of a born Texas fighter.

So Midnight said, 'Any man that wants to trade lead with me c'n do so right now. There ain't no takers?' His eyes lashed them with scorn. Suddenly, like greased lightning, twin Colts leapt into his hands. The crowd swayed back before the threat.

'Okay, then get movin'. Go on, the lot of you. Get away from that hoss an' let me through.'

They parted like butter yielding before the blade of a white-hot knife. One resolute man with two deadly guns had intimidated fifty times as many. And still not one of them dared to be first in reaching for his weapons; and the men in front whispered in agony to those behind, 'Fer Christ sake don't do nothin. *We'll* be first to stop lead, not you critters.'

When they were back from the rail,

Midnight walked slowly over and untied. They were waiting for him to vault into the saddle and turn and go helter-skelter down the street in a race against the lead they would immediately throw after him.

But he did nothing of the sort. Midnight had shot up too many Mexican border towns not to know all the answers.

He climbed without haste or fuss into the saddle — and his guns never moved from the direction of the crowd while he did so. Then, still without haste or fuss, he prodded his well-trained horse into moving step by step backwards until they were opposite a break between two frame buildings. Then, and only then, did he move quickly.

Like lightning his guns went away and he pulled his horse's head round and in a flash they were out of sight behind the building. Not a shot was fired after him. Every man in that crowd knew it would only have been so much wasted lead and powder — Midnight had been too slick for them.

And nobody came in pursuit, because Midnight looked too dangerous a man to meet out on the open prairie.

$$\star \quad \star \quad \star$$

Midnight knew where he was going. He went north until he came to the even smaller township of Old Bull's Skull — but it wasn't so small that it was without a telegraph office. There he dispatched a wire to their San Antonio office demanding an immediate Senate inquiry into the local ban on the import of barbed wire.

Then he remounted and set off at an easy lope back across the prairie, and yet still he did not head for the Ricketts' ranch. He was thinking of that word 'immediate' in his telegram, thinking that from what he knew of Senates, immediate could mean anything from three months to three years. The fight was on his own hands yet awhile . . .

His horse kept up that tireless lope for the next three hours, and then

Midnight turned down a wagon trail that went among trees that crowded a valley bottom. When he was through these trees he saw an old-style Texan loghouse before him — a typical cattleman's home, consisting of two rooms and the inevitable dog-run between them, and the usual outbuildings, all in rough-hewn, clay-packed logs.

The place was silent. He rode up, calling, then dismounted and took a seat on a bench within the shade of the dog-run and waited.

About an hour passed, and then a man came slowly up the hill from behind and entered the dog-run by the back way. Midnight was on his feet, facing him as he came in. He looked at the red clay on the man's boots and working jeans, then looked into a startled face and said, 'Howdy, Ben Coe. I never heard tell of gold in these parts.'

10

Ben Coe flushed under his dark skin. He seemed somehow furtive at being surprised in this manner. 'What're you doin' here, fencer?' he rasped.

Midnight calmly took a seat again and said, 'I came to see you, of course.'

Coe took down a scraper from a hook on the wall and began to dig the clay off his boot soles. He grunted surlily, 'What d'you want with me, Midnight?'

Midnight spoke straight. 'You hate my guts, Coe, because I'm now on the side of the fencers and you're at heart a fence buster. Okay, but I think you're a fair man and won't stand for no jiggery-pokery.'

Coe didn't look up.

'There's a hell of a lot of jiggery-pokery goin' on right now, Coe, and I want you to pitch in your hand to try'n stop it.'

Ben Coe's face came up flushed and angry. 'You want me to help you goddam fencers? Brother, you got a hope!'

Midnight sighed. 'I know. I guess it's a small hope. But — all right, I came hopin' against hope. Do you want to know what's happenin' now, Coe? What them blamed Eastern financiers are tryin' to do now in order to get a range war goin'?'

Coe shrugged, as if indifferent, but nevertheless his interest had been aroused, and he said, 'As you're here, you might as well tell me.'

So Midnight told him.

'They've bought the law. That's my guess, but I'll put my chips on it that my hunch is right. They've got around the sheriff — he's in their pocket right now.' His voice was harsh. He had no time for sheriffs who could be bought out of their job.

'Con Tierney's been bought?' Then Coe shrugged, and there was a sarcastic air to the movement, as if after all the news wasn't any great surprise to him.

154

'Tierney's been to tell us that runnin' wire into the county is causin' too much bother. It's got to stop, he says: an' he's put a ban on the import of wire into the county.'

Ben Coe was puzzled, just as they all had been puzzled by the manoeuvre. 'I don't understand. The Easterners want war on the range — stoppin' wire comin' in won't build the war up, will it?'

Midnight looked across at the distant hills, his eyes thoughtful. 'Maybe he doesn't think I'll accept the ban. Maybe he hopes to catch me bringing wire into the county — I don't know. There's a lot of maybes to this manoeuvre. It's deep, Coe, deep as the Rio Grande.'

'One thing I can see out of it all. If Tierney's been bought, he'll have to earn his money. He's bein' paid to ride agen me an' my friends, an' I guess that ef I don't give no trouble he'll invent some excuse to go for me. He'll come a-gunnin' — an' at his back he'll have a posse . . . '

Ben Coe said, softly, 'I'm beginnin'

to see daylight. Sure, I get it now. Tierney will swear in all the fence busters in his posse, and that'll include the Longhorn and the few paid trouble-makers the Easterners have shipped in. Sure, I get it now. Fence bustin's gonna be made lawful.'

'That's about it. They'll be able to tear down any fence they like, swearin' that the wire was imported in defiance of the sheriff's ban. And that will start war.'

He rounded on Ben Coe with unusual vigour. 'You know, in spite of what you and your friends say, most people want to see the range fenced in. They recognise that fencin' will be the makin' of the cattle country — '

'I don't agree with you,' said Coe harshly. 'Most people are agen fencin'.' But at the end of the abrupt sentence he looked quickly down at his soiled jeans and boots, and his manner became furtive again, as if he had remembered something that cast doubt upon his obstinate statement.

'No. Only a handful are agen it, and they're gettin' smaller an' smaller in number every day. The trouble is,' Midnight continued ironically, 'that little bunch o' hotheads make so much noise they sound a lot.'

They sat in silence for a while after that, and then Coe spoke. 'You've told me all this — now what do you expect me to do?'

Midnight shrugged. 'I don't rightly know. But I guess you've got influence among your fence-bustin' pals. Ef you went round an' told 'em what I've told you, maybe they'd think twice about runnin' alongside Sher'f Tierney, the Longhorn and friends. That way we'd keep trouble on the range to a minimum. Coe, I just don't want to see a lot of men shootin' things out — you c'n help by talkin' your side out of joinin' up with the sher'f.'

Coe said, obstinately, 'I ain't doin' any talkin'. I've got so much work on my hands, I can't go gallivantin' off for a day or two. The hell, why should I do it, just to help the blamed fencers?' he exploded angrily.

Midnight sighed. He knew he had lost. 'There's a lot o' mule in you, Coe. You'll come round in the end because you're a fair man, but I only hope you don't leave it till too late.'

'I won't change my mind.' Coe was stripping off his sweaty shirt.

Midnight untied his horse and swung aboard. Then he looked down and said, 'When you find that gold, Coe, come'n see me. There's a ban on imports, but' — he winked broadly — 'I'll fix you with as much barbed wire as you want.'

The expression on Coe's bushed and angry face was that of a man who has thought to be clever but sees now he has been found out. For it was obvious that Midnight knew it wasn't gold he was digging for — it was . . . water.

★ ★ ★

Sandy must have been looking out for him, because as soon as he showed above the bare hill north of the Ricketts' place, she jumped for a horse and came galloping to meet him. She was riding bareback, he noticed, as she came pelting up the trail towards him, and his heart approved of the way she so easily sat her long-striding horse.

The men on the rails waved as they came in, and Wee Jock got down and said, 'I'll tend to your hoss, Tom. You go git yourself some grub an' a rest.'

Old man Ricketts was in the rough but comfortable main room, and with him a lean, dark-bearded cattleman. Ricketts said, 'How d'you go on today, Tom?'

Midnight sank into a chair with a little, non-committal shrug of his shoulders. He didn't intend to open his mouth in the presence of strangers. Ricketts understood and didn't press the question. Instead he half-turned towards his guest and smiled.

'You've got another customer for your wire, Tom — Oklahoma Smith, a neighbour o' mine.'

It startled Midnight. He came across with hand outstretched but all the same he was uncertain. He said, 'The last time I heard your name you were a fence buster.'

Oklahoma took the hand saying, with some sheepishness, 'Sure, but don't we all start out as fence busters?'

Midnight said seriously, 'I guess so. But how come you changed your mind so quick?'

Sandy spoke for the man. 'I guess I changed it for him, Tom.' He looked at her in astonishment. 'Sure, I did. I thought he'd be another customer for you, and jingo we need more custom, don't we?'

Midnight sank back and drank the refreshing coffee. 'Now, hold your hosses an' tell me how you made Oklahoma Smith a fencer.'

'I remembered what my dad used to say. He used to stamp and rave that Oklahoma Smith had the best range in the country and didn't know it. He swore that under Oklahoma's land was

160

so much waer it could flood Texas — and Oklahoma as well.'

Oklahoma interrupted, 'He used to come an' tell me that an' I never believed him, but goldarn it if the old fellar wasn't dead shootin' all the time. The trouble was, while there was free range and some water around I didn't want the trouble of sinking wells. I guess diggin' ain't in my line, and well-sinkin's apt to be mighty expensive.'

'But I went over a few days ago and I talked very severely with Mr. Smith.' It was Sandy speaking again. 'This time he was willing to listen because most of the water's been fenced against him, and what little he's got will dry up any time now. He took a shot in digging in order to keep his cattle alive, and — well, it seems to have come off.'

Oklahoma rose, he was so jubilant. 'By God, Midnight, it has come off, too, and so easily. Right where old man Addason allus said it would be. There's a deep depression back of a salt lick; old

Will used to say nature had pretty near dug the well for me. You know, we dug for a couple of days, got down about thirty feet, when suddenly the water came up in a spout.'

'An artesian well, huh?'

'It sure is. That depression's now a lake, an' the water's comin' up so fast, jeosophat, I'm gonna build myself an ark pretty dam'n quick!'

They all laughed, and then Midnight said dryly, 'So now you've got all the water you want, you're aimin' to fence it and keep it all to yourself?' That was the way it was, he figgered.

Oklahoma said, 'Maybe it looks bad, but I don't see what else I c'n do. There's barely enough grass to support my own herd now; ef other people's cattle come up for water, I guess we'll be down to sand within a month, and then the land'll go to desert. Now that fencin's started, I guess we'll all have to fence up, so that's why I came.'

Ricketts growled, 'He's right, Midnight. Over-grazin's as bad as bein' without water, so far as Oklahoma's land is concerned. If it's looked after, it can become fine cattle country, but he can't look after it without fences.'

Midnight sighed. He badly wanted sleep. 'Okay, then tell me how much wire you want, sign the order, and let me hit the haybag.'

Ricketts, the girl and Oklahoma exchanged quick glances. Midnight was too tired to notice it. Then Ricketts spoke. 'Before you talk about takin' orders, Tom, there's something Oklahoma wants to know. What're you gonna use for wire, now you can't import it into the area?'

Midnight clambered to his feet. He was suddenly awfully, awfully tired.

'That all?' he drawled. Sandy was watching him, wondering if he could get around this obstacle as he had got round others in the past. He knew she was worrying, waiting anxiously, so he said, 'Guess my pardner, Miss Addason, will take your order while I get some sleep.'

'But the wire — ?' Sandy spoke breathlessly, not understanding.

'It'll be here when it's wanted,' said Midnight confidently, and then he went and slept like a man who has done good work but knows he can do better.

11

Hot beans and bacon and even hotter coffee, and Midnight felt capable of another twenty-four hours in the saddle. He was, in any event, first man to stir on the Ricketts' place, and when Sandy came in he had already break-fasted and was patiently awaiting her arrival.

Sandy began immediately. 'You might as well know it, Tom, but we all decided against putting up wire on the Smith place just yet awhile.'

Midnight's chin came up stubbornly. 'Why? You scared or somep'n?'

She nodded. 'Yes, Tom, I'm scared. You don't understand — Oklahoma Smith's spread strikes right across the range. If that's fenced off it puts a barrier clean across the Big Valley, and the cattlemen south of it will have a long drive round when it comes to moving their herds. They won't stand for that.'

'It's Smith's land, don't forget,' said Midnight softly. 'An' drivin' cattle round it ain't as bad as it sounds. I guess it can't put more'n half a day on to any well-run drive. Sure that'll make 'em mad, but what's Smith to do — leave his land open and watch it go to ruin to provide a straight road through to the railhead? Let 'em get mad. Maybe we'll get a bit mad, too.'

'You mean you're goin' ahead with the fencin'?' Old man Ricketts was in the doorway.

Midnight nodded. 'If Smith's willin'.'

Ricketts said, 'So long as you know that stickin' that fence up will start trouble, I'm willin' to talk him into it. Now tell me what you're gonna do for wire?'

Midnight said, calmly, 'Smuggle it in.'

Sandy gasped, 'Smuggle in tons and tons of barbed wire? Why, Tom, they'll be watching the only road in and you'll never get it through.'

Midnight rose and went to the window. 'See them hills? Felipe tells me the first road ever made through these parts was a military route that cut bang over the top of them. He says in this dry weather that old trail should take the wagons. So I'm off right now to San Antonio. That means three day's ridin', then it'll take eight or nine days to come back with the freight. When we get near to the Passender Cutting, Felipe and the boys will be waitin' to take the wagons up the old military trail. I guess we'll have to fight every yard of the way over the hills, but I reckon to do it.'

'Fight?' Old man Ricketts' eyes bushed interrogatively.

Midnight shook his head. 'Not that kind o' fightin', I hope. I mean a fight agen rocks an' slopes an' a trail choked with sand an' bush. Nope.' He shook his head decisively. 'That's one thing we mustn't have — trouble with any people. Everyone must watch their step an' be good boys. No brawls, no fightin', no hard words an' swearin', even, I guess. That sheriff's lookin' for an excuse to move in on us, an' I don't want to find myself buckin' agen a posse of indignant if misguided citizens. Some day I'll be wantin' to sell 'em all wire,' he ended humorously.

Then Smith came in, rubbing the soap out of his beard from a sluice in a tub round the back. They talked for a while, then he nodded and signed the order form. But across the order he wrote, 'Conditional upon the vendor providing protection while the fence is being erected.'

He threw down the old-fashioned quill pen and said, 'How you're gonna do it ain't none of my business, Midnight, but I ain't in no position to tackle a range war myself. I don't pay a cent until thar's a fence round my place, an' that means you gotta do the fightin' for me until it's finished. After that I guess it's up to me to look after my own property, which I reckon to do.'

168

There was a shout outside just then. Wee Jock McCraw came running in on his stumpy legs. 'Someone's comin',' he called. 'An' I reckon he's in a powerful hurry, too.'

They went out on to the broad, shaded veranda, and looked up the winding, dusty hill trail that led to the town of Devine. A cloud of yellow dust hung over it, a couple of miles away, and it was moving fast and coming in closer. Sharp eyes detected one rider only.

Midnight slung his legs across the rail and spoke to Oklahoma as though nothing had happened to interrupt their conversation. 'You leave the fightin' to me an' my men,' he said easily. 'I want that wire up because it'll bring matters to a head. If we win out, I guess the trouble'll subside an' then I'll clean up that fortune my uncle promised with quick sales to every galoot who owns land this side o' the Nueces River.'

Smith watched that approaching

figure and said, 'Ef you win out.' He turned to the big cowpuncher. 'You sure got confidence, Midnight, but I guess you'll need all of it. Thar's a lot of meanness felt over this wirin', an' when they see my land bein' fenced, jeosophat, but the lid'll go off! People like Jim Daly, Paul Kiplock, Sadd Towers, Ben Coe an' Paul Reiten — they've all got land south o' mine, an' by god they'll bring their men in agen me when they see the fence go up.'

Midnight stood up. That solitary horseman was crossing the gravel of the dried-up watercourse now and would be up to them in half a minute.

'Ben Coe?' His eyes were speculative. 'You know what, Oklahoma? That guy must have heard of all that water you've got on your land, an' right now he's busy digging holes all over his spread, I reckon. Ef he don't find water, I guess it'll make him madder than ever. Ef he does, you bet he'll forget he ever was a fence buster, an' he'll come up an' sign a form for a load o' wire.'

And yet, thinking of Coe, he couldn't help feeling disappointed. He'd gone to Coe to gain an ally, but Coe's last words hadn't been friendly. They'd have listened to Coe, he thought; if Coe had told them not to be suckers, that they were being used to further the ends of unscrupulous Eastern financiers, they'd have been abrupt at any approaches by Sheriff Tierney or the Longhorn or his followers. He shrugged. It looked, from what Smith said, more likely he would find Coe in the van of any action against him.

Oklahoma Smith said, 'This looks like Dandy Kiplock ... no, it's his brother, Paul. Reckon I'll keep out o' sight while he's here. It'd only start people talking prematurely if they knew I'd been to the Ricketts place.'

Ricketts said, 'I reckon that's no bad idea, Oklahoma. Paul don't look good-tempered to me.'

Paul Kiplock came stiffly down from his saddle and walked up to the veranda. He ignored Midnight's men who had sauntered casually up, and addressed himself to their leader.

'You, Midnight, what have you done with my brother?'

Big Tom Midnight came slowly down the veranda steps towards him. Paul Kiplock wasn't half his height, but he was an aggressive, bantam-cock of a fellow, and he was playing with his gun belt as though ready to start trouble any minute.

Midnight said, 'I don't know your brother. I ain't never seen him, that I know of. Why should I know where he is?'

Kiplock shouted, 'The hell you know what's happened to him! He ain't been seen since a coupla nights ago.'

'He was with the fence busters?' Midnight's voice was sardonic. 'We didn't ask him to come trouble-makin'. Ef he got more than he bargained for, that ain't none of my calculatin'.'

Kiplock went on shouting, 'He ain't bin seen since, an' we've searched that hillside high an' low an' he ain't thar.

You done somethin' to him an' got him hid away, you dog-gone — '

Big Tom jumped him. He got there just as the enraged Kiplock's hand was reaching for a gun. Midnight's big body crashed into the smaller man and flattened him to the ground. In a flash Midnight was up on his feet, Kiplock's gun in his hand. He rammed it into his own belt, then bent and hefted the surprised cattle-owner to his feet.

Before Kiplock knew what was happening he found himself propelled by the seat of his pants and the scruff of his neck, loping in great strides towards his horse. A couple of yards short of it, Midnight picked him up and hurled him into the saddle.

'Friend,' said Midnight, and he wasn't even breathing heavily, 'thar's people just waitin' for a chance to jump us. I reckon if I'd let you get your gun someone'd have shot you down, an' that would have been a good excuse for Sheriff Tierney to come a-buttin' in.

Thank Tierney for savin' your bad-tempered life, hombre,' he ended. Then he stuck the gun into the back of Kiplock's belt, banged the rump of the horse with a heavy hand, and sent it galloping back along the trail towards Devine.

When Tom Midnight turned he found a wide smile on every man's face. Old man Ricketts called down from the veranda, 'Boy, you sure know how to look after yourself!' And one of his men said, 'Ef I could move half as quick as that big lug, I'd fancy myself agen lightning.'

But Midnight wasn't listening. He was pulling on his gloves, and his eyes followed that small, bouncing figure galloping through the dust towards Devine.

Suddenly he looked at his men and said, 'That still didn't answer a very important question, I guess. *What happened — to Dandy Kiplock?*'

He was still quietly worrying as he cantered northwards, to join the old military road that Felipe said was good enough to take wheeled traffic. It was at once a survey and also a means of circumventing a hostile little cattle town called Devine.

Sandy rode with him right into the hills. When she saw the military road she shuddered. 'How you expect to bring those big wagons along this track, I don't know, Tom.'

He looked at the twisting trail, at times riding close to precipitous drops; he saw the appallingly steep shale-treacherous gradients, and the places where boulders had fallen into the passes and trees had become uprooted by gales and were across the way. He looked, considered, and was not down-hearted. When they were right through the neck of the hills, and he could see the distant wooded defile that was the Passender Cutting, he said, 'Guess we c'n make it, Sandy.'

They halted. This was where they had to part.

Midnight looked again back along

that trail. 'All told it amounts to around fifteen miles only,' he said. 'We'll make it in two days, you see if we don't.'

Sandy said, mournfully, 'I don't want to hear how long it'll take you to get through that pass. I — I just don't know how I'm going to last without seeing you for nearly a fortnight.'

Midnight shook his head resignedly. 'Honey, you're so shameless, the way you say things to a fellar, goldarn it, you'll have me doin' things next.'

'Such as?' Her eyes were delighted, challenging.

He leaned across. His lips were very close to her soft red ones, parted slightly so that the even white of her teeth just showed. He said, softly, 'Kissin' you, honey.'

And when he had kissed her he said, 'You stop chasin' me in this unmaidenly manner, Sandy Addason. You'll sure have me hog-tied an' thrown into matrimony, the rate you're goin' on.'

Sandy threw back her head and laughed joyously. 'Oh, Tom, that's been

176

my intention almost from the first time I saw you. And it's no use, you won't get away from me.'

When he went on alone there was an expression on his face which said that maybe he didn't mind being hog-tied by bonny Sandy Addason . . .

★   ★   ★

Close on two weeks later a train of seven heavily loaded wagons came creaking down the trail towards the inviting green defile that was the Passender Cutting. The oxen were weary, because it was near to the end of the day, and the teamsters were jaded by the sun and fatigued by the exertion of keeping the wheels rolling. Midnight rode loosely, slumped in his saddle, because he had been trying to force the pace all the way, and when a wheel had stuck he'd been down first to try to get the thing to move again. He was feeling the strain, this late afternoon.

A couple of miles from the pass, a

lone rider came out and galloped down to meet him. He spurred forward, thinking it might be Sandy — pretty sure it would be — but it turned out to be that dwarfed little man, Wee Jock McCraw. He hid his disappointment; he had done little else but think of the girl ever since the moment he had left her.

Jock said, 'You're right on time, Tom. An' we've got the trail pretty clear, so we'll be over and on Ricketts' land within two days, just as Sandy told us you reckoned on.'

They walked their horses ahead of the dust storm that the lowing oxen kicked up. Midnight said, 'Everything okay, Jock?'

Wee Jock said, 'Oh, sure,' but he was uneasy.

'No trouble, no rumpus with the sher'f or anythin'?' Suddenly Midnight knew there was something seriously wrong.

Jock said, 'We ain't seen nothin' o' the sher'f, an' thars been no rumpus of any kind.'

'But somethin's worryin' you, Jock,' said Midnight gently. 'Come on, fellar, come out with it. Why keep it back?'

Wee Jock sighed. 'I jes' nacherly hate to tell you, Tom. Thar's been no trouble but — we found Dandy Kiplock!'

Midnight knew by the way he said it that there was something important about the finding of Dandy — and pretty bad, too. He said, 'So?'

'He was found a coupla days back by some of Ricketts' men out roundin' up strays to get 'em into the wire.'

'The way you talk, Dandy Kiplock was — dead?'

Wee Jock spat decisively. 'Ef he warn't, then he ougta be. He'd bin tied up in a tree ever since the fight a coupla weeks back, and — he didn't have a scalp.'

'Scalped?' Big Tom's mind was racing. 'That's an Injun trick, an' so's tyin' a body up a tree.' He reined in. 'What did you do about it, Jock?'

Jock said, 'We didn't do nothin'. We didn't know what to figger out, at first.

179

But Sandy did. When she got the news she went inside to her room. Next thing we see she's got a Derringer in her hand an' she's walkin' across to where Felipe's standing against the south corral.'

'Felipe!' That was the thought that had instantly sprung to Big Tom's mind. And then he panicked for about the first time in his life. He couldn't see Sandy among those men in the defile. He asked quickly, 'Did anythin' happen to Sandy? Quick, tell me, Jock!'

But Jock spat contemptuously again and said, 'That gal sure c'n look after herself. She stood in front of Felipe an' said, 'You did it, Felipe. You went an' scalped that poor fellar, you danged Comanche.' Well, maybe not in quite them words.'

'And then?'

'Felipe tried to jump her, just as he'd seen you jump the other Kiplock that day, only Sandy wasn't bluffin' an' she wasn't slow with her finger, either. She jes' blew a chunk of flesh outa Felipe's shoulder, an' it kind o' set him back a bit till we had chance to get over to him.'

Midnight breathed out a long sigh of relief. 'Thank God she wasn't hurt . . . What did you do with Felipe?'

'We put a bit o' bandage on the fellar to keep him alive till you came back an' said what had to be done with him, and then we stuck him in a 'dobe hut without windows. We're danged ef we know what to do about the hombre.'

'Dandy Kiplock?'

'We buried him where we'd found him.'

'Why?'

Wee Jock gestured helplessly with his stunted arms. 'What could we do with him? We couldn't go an' hand him over to the sher'f, could we? C'n you imagine the shindig ef the town had got to know that one of Midnight's men had scalped a fence buster? I guess the whole county'd have come over an' steam-rollered us an' the Ricketts' ranch clean outa existence.'

Midnight nodded. 'Guess you're right, Jock. But — What'n heck are we gonna do about it? We can't just say nothin' about Dandy, an' ef we say somethin' they'll see he ain't got no scalp an' then the ruckus'll begin. An' Felipe — doggone it, we can't let that heathen get away with his Injun tricks,' he swore, and he was thinking of an old couple who had also been found scalped not long ago. Thinking it was time retribution came good and finally to the arrogant young breed.

It was Jock for once who was able to give advice. He said, 'Let's get this blamed wire on to Ricketts' land afore we start to think o' them things.' And because there was, after all, nothing else they could do about the matter, Midnight nodded in agreement.

His men rose to greet him as he came slowly up. There were six of them — seven with Wee Jock. They looked to have been working hard, too, on that trail-clearing job, and Midnight decided they would make camp early, to get the

182

maximum amount of rest before tackling that last hard section over into Ricketts' land.

'Hyar,' he said to their greetings. 'I'm sure glad to see you. The road's hotter'n hell, an' I'll trade you a team o' oxen for a pair o' mules any day.' Midnight wasn't born to be a teamster, not of horned beasts, anyway.

Joe Culloch squinted up and said, 'Reckon by that you an' the beasts c'n do with a rest, huh? Waal, through the pass is good, sweet water an' plenty grass, an' I reckon that's the place to camp for the night.'

Midnight said, shortly, 'Sounds good, Joe.' And to the teamsters he shouted. 'Keep 'em rollin'; another coupla miles an' then we camp.'

That was inspiring news, and men shouted and cursed at stubborn, slow-moving oxen, and cracked great long whips over their heads in order to get better pace out of them. The pace quickened as the oxen entered the welcome damp greenness of the Passender Cutting.

Luxuriant shrubs and grasses grew close up to the trail, tempting the weary beasts to grab succulent mouthfuls as they passed, while the way was cool because of the shadows of thickly-leaved elms and sycamores and the tall-towering cedars. Soon they were at the end of the defile, and at the beginning of the old military route over the hills. But that was far enough for one day, and when they came to the fresh, sweet water that Joe Culloch had mentioned, they made camp for the night.

Morning, cool because of a quick easterly breeze but promising another blazing hot day, came all too soon; but with the first light of dawn Midnight was striding up and down the camp, shouting the laggards out of bed and getting the train in motion once again.

Now, so near to Devine, he wanted to make the last section in record style. The less time they were on the trail, the less chance there was of being seen with that suspicious cargo.

184

It was back-breaking work, wrestling those wagons up the sharp gradients and around tricky bends. Time after time the whole train would come to a halt until Midnight and his men hitched on to the first wagon with ropes and put their strength into hauling it over the worst places . . . and then the second, third, and right to the last.

By midday their shirts were black with sweat and sticking unpleasantly to their bodies, and the dust had risen and was caked on their perspiring faces. The dust was never out of their eyes and nostrils and mouths all that day. They came to hate the stuff, and when it came up particularly bad, so the curses of the men rose proportionately.

By late afternoon Midnight stood his horse back of the trail and watched while the teamsters flogged their tired beasts into a final spurt of effort that was to carry them that last mile before camp was made for the night. He was thinking, 'At least it'll be cool and pleasant, sleepin' out in these hills,' when another sound came to his ears over the noise of the moving train.

Someone was galloping fast and furiously down that rocky trail towards them. Midnight kicked spurs into his horse and went racing up the trail away from the wagons. As he went he sent out a call, and immediately seven riders came streaking all along the sides of the train after him.

At the bend in the trail they saw the approaching rider . . . then saw others, as if in pursuit of the first.

And Midnight saw the gleam of golden sun upon dark, coppery bodies and knew them for Indians.

Then the first rider was standing in the stirrups and shouting glad welcome at sight of them. Sandy! Sandy with her hair blowing back in long streamers, and her hat caught round her neck by the strap and bouncing against her shoulders.

She came into the group with a rush, and she was so glad that as she came level with Midnight she held out both arms for him to take her, which he did, so that her horse continued without her until it halted, head drooping from fatigue.

Sandy gasped, 'I was coming to meet you. I ran into an Indian camp right across the trail — I was on it before I knew what was happening, and all I could do was race right through it. A few of them set off after me . . .'

The Indians had pulled back their ponies, so viciously that the screams of pain came floating to their ears as the beasts were savagely hauled around. For a few seconds the Indians halted and held palaver, while Midnight and his little group of men stood and watched. The Indians were rather the greater in number, but not in sufficient force to encourage them to open up an attack on the hardy Texans.

After a while they all turned, as if at an order, and went trotting back the way they had come.

Midnight wheeled and rode towards the leading wagon. When he was close up he raised the palm of his hand, then circled it. The leading teamster knew what that meant, though he hadn't received such a signal in years.

Indians!

So they wheeled into a big circle, just as the old covered-wagon pioneers had circled up at nights against a possible Indian attack.

Midnight and his men rode in with the news. Then Midnight said, 'Mex, you, Fred an' Skippy get ready to go scoutin' with me. I guess we'd better find out what we're up agen.'

Midnight got a drink for Sandy before moving out. He also tried to find out more about the Indians. She wasn't able to help much. 'They've got tepees and squaws and papooses,' she said. 'Could be there's a couple of hundred all told.'

'That makes maybe fifty to eighty fightin' men,' said Midnight, then took a long, deep draught himself. Then he told her, 'You didn't oughta come by yourself, Sandy. These hill trails ain't never safe for a lone gal, I reckon.'

She said, simply, 'I had to come. Felipe. He got away. I guess one of Mr. Ricketts' Mex servants was talked into helpin' him. And that boy hates us. Tom, hates us because I shot him an' hurt him. *And the last we heard of him he was heading straight for Devine.*'

12

Midnight meditated against the side of his tired horse for a moment, then swung into the saddle, and there was that old, fighting look on his face again. 'Let's go see 'bout these hyar Injuns,' he drawled. 'Then we'll see what the escape of Felipe means to us, huh?'

Cautiously they rode up the trail, rifles held across their saddles before them, Colts slung forward ready for close work if it came.

Then they ran bang into the Indian camp; just as Sandy had done. They were in a widening of the track, where another trail joined from the south and cut right across on its northward journey. And plainly the Indians hadn't expected them to come so quickly and so boldly after them.

They were congregated in a wide circle right where the cross trails met.

All that Midnight could see were the squaws and children on the fringe of the circle, but he knew that within would be the chiefs and their braves holding palaver.

He motioned his men to get back under cover — they hadn't been spotted and there was no sense in drawing attention to themselves unnecessarily.

King Cass, close up with Midnight, said, 'Comanches, huh?'

Midnight said, 'They've got no dogs in their camp — pack dogs; so that means they're not Apaches. Probably a Penateka tribe of the Comanches.'

Cass spat. 'So we know what to expect.'

Midnight said, 'The Penatekas are the most savage of all the Comanches. An' they're right bang in our way.'

He was looking at the siting of the Indian camp as Cass said, 'I heerd tell that the Comanches is talkin' war up at Wichita. I reckon this party is aimin' to go up an' talk war with 'em.'

Most of the Penatekas' tepees were set up where the broad south trail climbed to cross their own, though a few warriors had set up tents right at the crossing. It was wide, there, and Midnight noted that the tepees were set back close against the rock wall of the hillside. He rubbed his bristling chin for a moment while he took in all the details of that thronging valley trail, then turned to go.

It was getting dark when they arrived back at camp, for the sun had dropped behind the mountain range while they were riding in from the Indian lodges. A big fire was blazing, making a cheerful glow to welcome them. There was food and coffee waiting, and willing hands to take their horses.

Midnight said, 'They're Comanches — probably Penatekas. That means they won't attack during darkness, so — we live till tomorrow, anyway.' But he grinned as he spoke, and they knew that Big Tom Midnight intended to go on living for a lot more tomorrows.

Sandy was sitting close to him, feeling glad of the warmth of the fire because so high in the mountains the evening was proving cool. She asked, 'And tomorrow? Will they attack?'

Midnight finished his coffee and reached for his makings. 'Ef they don't,' he said, 'I've made a mistake an' they're not Comanches.'

'An' they are Comanches,' supplemented Mex Jacinto. 'That, or I'm a liar.'

Midnight thought, 'We're bottled up in this pass. All they need do is sit across it an' starve us out.' Not that Comanches would be so patient; much more likely they would snipe from a distance, interspersing such conduct with sudden, swift charges on their wild little ponies. With such a force against them, probably three of four times their number and with the possibility of reinforcements still to come, it could only be a question of time before the white men were wiped out.

'Can we fight our way through, Tom?'

abruptly demanded King Cass.

Midnight shook his head. 'The next two miles of trail is particularly bad, King; it gets narrower round the bend, so that them varmints need only build a wall of boulders to stop us completely. An' then they'll climb the cliffs an' just pour lead down into us, I reckon.'

He looked at Sandy and said, 'I wish you weren't with us, honey. Things sure look tough . . .'

Sandy took his hand and said, simply, 'Thank God I'll be with my man whatever happens,' and at that he put his arm round her shoulders and drew her to him.

Midnight lay down, but his face was to the fire, watching the dying embers and the occasional burst of flame that weakly threw up a cascade of sparks. He found himself thinking, 'Now, if them blamed wagons could fly as easy as them sparks we could jump right over the heads of them Injuns while they're sleepin.'

And suddenly he sat up, his fists

clenched, his eyes sparkling. 'By God,' he exclaimed, 'it was starin' me in the face all the time. Why didn't I think of it. That's what we'll do . . . '

He let the camp sleep for a further four hours, then with still three hours to go before dawn, he roused them from their sleep. He begrudged even those four hours, but he knew that the oxen, if not the men, must have a rest from their labours. Some of the beasts had hardly been able to stand when camp was struck that night, and there was a hard task ahead for them.

There was surprise in the voices of the men when he shook them roughly and told them to get the train moving. He'd made coffee, so they were able to gulp down the scalding hot, refreshing drink, but that was all the breakfast he gave them time for.

He put the situation bluntly. 'We can't go back, because them blamed Comanches'd be after us like lightnin'. We can't hole up here, because we couldn't hold this place half a day with all that cover for the varmints. An' ef we wait till daylight an' then try'n break through, they'll stop us up the narrow trail where it'll be even hotter for us. So — what do we do?'

There was silence.

Midnight continued, 'You know, I got to thinkin' what we might do, and it seemed our best bet was to start up now and walk right through that Injun camp while it's dark.'

It startled the men, and they didn't all get the idea at first. 'You mean, leave the wagons an' sneak past 'em?' Fred Callason was surprised.

'No, sirree,' retorted Midnight. 'We came so far with the blamed wire, we're goin' through with it. And I think we can go through with it.'

'But they'll hear the wagons — '

'So what? I got to thinking all I knew about the Comanches, lyin' by the fire just now. They hate the dark. They think that night is a great black snake that gets its grip on the world every few hours. They think that if anything happens to 'em in the dark an' they die, the snake will swallow their spirit and they will never visit the Happy Hunting Grounds where all braves aspire to go.'

'It sounds risky, I know,' he argued. 'But what else is there we can do, if we're not to abandon the wire — '

Someone called, 'Blamed ef we're gonna do that for some pesky Injuns. Me, I'm fer tryin' Tom's way first.'

Midnight quietened the growl of approval. 'They're cowards in the dark, these Comanches. They won't come out an' fight — though after daybreak it'll be very much different,' he added grimly. 'Well, the thing is to put the fear of death into them varmints, to drive 'em back from the trail.'

'They'll hear us comin'. Okay, let 'em hear us. When you start up, make such a noise they'll think it's a train-load of banshees goin' through, savvy? Scream, shout, do anything you like — but put the fear of death into 'em. They're superstitious, they won't stand around to see what all the noise is about.'

Joe Culloch said, 'I'm on, Tom. I guess you're right about Comanches not fightin' in the dark. But, look, we gotta start the wheels rollin' right away. It's two miles to the top of the pass after we've got past the Injuns — an' it ain't no Galveston boulevard goin' down the other side.'

'And it'll be light by the time we're over the top, and then the Injuns'll be after us.' Midnight, better than Joe Culloch, knew the urgency of the moment. 'All the same,' he told them, 'don't start right away. I'm goin' ahead. Give me twenty minutes' start, then come after me.'

Sandy's voice came in a whisper from the darkness as he strode over to his horse. 'Oh, Tom, must you leave me?'

He swung into his saddle then bent over her. 'Sure, honey. I got an idea to help us when we run into daylight — an' them pesky Injuns.'

'An idea? What?'

'Call it insurance,' he grinned in the darkness. 'Yeah, that's what it is. I'm takin' out a bit of insurance, I reckon, to give us time on the way down.'

He bent swiftly, felt her arms go round his neck, felt the softness of her lips and the warmth of her breath on his cheek as he kissed her.

As he rode he wondered if he'd be able to spot that distinctive tepee in the very short time he had before the wagons started rolling. If he didn't . . .

At the appointed time the leading teamster stood on the board and sent his long whip snaking out across the broad patient backs of his team. There was a crack like a rifle discharging, and the report was taken up in echo after echo along the rocky-walled passage ahead of them.

At once Wee Jock McCraw threw back his puckish face and screamed to the night sky. 'Yee-ee-ee-ow!' At which every man-jack there raised his voice and added it to the blood-curdling din. If Midnight wanted noise, he was going to get noise!

It was startling, terrifying to the

beasts, and there was sudden pandemonium and panic among them. Strength was back in their limbs after the brief rest they'd had, and they threw all their weight into pulling those wagons into movement. The big, iron-shod wheels turned and screams rose in protest from the heavily laden axles, and then the oxen began to bellow in fright at the rude shattering of the night's silence.

Midnight heard it, and by the time he was in the heart of the Indian camp and he'd killed one man already.

The light-sleeping Indians were out of their tepees in an instant, startled, suspicious and apprehensive. Midnight heard them as he lay back of one ornate tepee.

Then he heard them start to call for their chief, but he didn't answer and he seemed to have run away, and that set up a panic. As the sound of the train came closer, the milling, leaderless mob retreated back among their tents along the rocky, southern trail. And there they stood still until the groaning wagons and the shrill-whooping teamsters and cowboys rode up to the crossing. Then they fled in superstitious terror, taking their wives and papooses and livestock with them.

But the wagons simply rolled straight onwards, still following the curving, uphill trail.

When they had gone past there were cries — 'Where's Tom? Anyone seen Midnight?' And Sandy's anxious voice was lifted with the rest.

He came suddenly galloping in from among the Indian tepees. He rode up to the last wagon and tipped a bundle inside, and then came up the line to show himself. The sky was lighter now, and they could see the grin on his face.

He called, 'Look like we done it, boys. We're through — now all we've got to do is stick ahead o' them varmints an' not let 'em get across the trail in front of us agen. And I got an insurance policy now, good for maybe a coupla hours when we most need it. Reckon we'll see the Ricketts' land under our wheels afore the sun's down this evening.'

And then they tore into that last gradient — it was a race against exhaustion and a race against the sun, clambering up towards the eastern horizon.

They beat it to the top of the pass. One moment the weight was on the shoulders of the tired beasts; the next the teamsters were standing on their brakes and hollering warnings as the wagons began a mad slide down a slope like the side of a house.

They were half a mile down the western slope of the hill, with night mist dissolving in the warming air, when disaster overtook them. Suddenly the leading wagon ran off the trail, where it narrowed at a sharp bend round a bluff. The team was safe, and stood panting great gouts of steamy breath, but the huge, lumbering wagon lay across the track with one front wheel overhanging the edge of a ninety-foot drop.

Midnight came flying up on his horse

and inspected the scene in the yellowing, strengthening light now flooding up from the east. The rim of the red morning sun was just showing now.

He said, in disgust, 'What a damn' thing to happen. It'll take us an hour to get that wheel up on to the track. An' that gives them Injuns plenty chance to get their wits back an' come a-huntin' us.'

In one hour they could have been several miles nearer home . . .

They worked frantically, unhitching the team from the second wagon and roping it to the rear of the leading freighter; then men rocked against the thick-spoked man-high wheels in a desperate effort to pull the truck on to four wheels again.

It never moved an inch.

So Midnight reluctantly said, 'That means we gotta unload her. She's too heavy for us to budge. Every man to it.'

His men jumped into that wagon like cats, rolled back the canvas cover and started to heft the heavy coils of wire over the side. It was back-breaking work, a race against time; and the sun was up now and the heat seemed to roll in intense waves over the arid, baked-yellow hills and on to them. Midnight was in with them, stripped to the waist, his brown, well-muscled body rolling with sweat as he shoved in the short unloading bars, then tipped the coils over the side.

The wagon was nearly empty when one of the rear-guards that Midnight had posted came flying recklessly down the rocky trail towads the last of the wagons. A shout down the line for Midnight. It came up as a message, 'The Injuns are on the move!'

Midnight vaulted over the side and grabbed his guns which had been hanging from a wheel hub. As he was buckling them on, he shouted orders.

'My men come with me!' Over the side they tumbled in a mad scramble for guns and horses. Sandy was holding his ready. Seconds counted. 'You — to the tough teamsters — get that wagon back on the road an' load it — every blamed bale, an' don't go kickin' none over the edge.' He knew teamsters by now. 'When you're ready, get movin' an' make the best time you can. We'll hold up them Injuns for a few hours an' give you a chance to make the plain.'

He saw Sandy turn and her trousered legs with their fringed buckskin pelted down the line for her horse. She was up in a flash. Sandy was as game for a scrap as any of the men. Old Walt Rath's Derringer was in her small, gloved hand. Midnight beckoned and she galloped down the line after him to the last wagon. He clambered aboard, calling her to bring her horse alongside. She saw him bend, and the muscles of his bare arms and torso ballooned up as he heaved and brought into sight a long blanket-wrapped object.

Sandy exclaimed, 'What on earth, Tom — '

Then Tom swung it across her saddle-bow. He jumped from the tailboard plumb into his own saddle, shouting, 'When the wagons roll, Sandy, you don't go with 'em. Stay here until I come back for you. An' use that gun o' yours ef you need to. 'Bye, honey.'

The little cavalcade went racing past and away, leaving her astride her horse close by the last of the wagons. She watched them go, then looked at the long, rolled-up object across the saddle in front of her.

After a while curiosity grew, and with the Derringer she poked back a loose end of the blanket. A gasp of horror came to her lips.

For a head had twisted round to gaze up at her — a savage, copper-faced Indian lay glaring up from inside that fold of blanket.

13

A quarter of a mile back, a series of dry water-courses broke into the main trail valley from either side. Midnight sent the two Callason brothers up a left divide; almost opposite he posted Wee Jock McCraw and Skippy Playfellow. The four men strung out, then dismounted and holed-up behind boulders. Their job was to prevent unmounted Indians from encircling the stranded wagons by clambering across the hillsides parallel to the track. With their Winchesters they would put up a formidable resistance.

A little farther up the track they came upon Mex Jacinto and Joe Culloch. They were sitting their horses across the trail, their Winchesters tucked under their arms, ready for action.

And a hundred yards away, a mob of mounted, war-painted Indians was approaching.

Midnight and King Cass joined them, and the four men sat silently, watching the slowly approaching, suspicious Indians. Midnight growled, 'There's a lot. Reckon some more must've joined 'em this mornin'.' Fully a hundred braves were on the trail, half of them mounted.

Midnight stirred. 'Minutes count,' he said. 'I'm goin' forward to make talk with the varmints. I'll keep 'em talkin' as long as I can.'

Then he spurred forward, his right hand raised to show that it was empty. Thirty yards from his men, he pulled up and lifted both hands to show that he had no weapons in them. The Indians stopped and their chiefs conferred together.

After a minute, however, a chieftain moved out to meet him. He had the full-feathered head-dress of a chief, though Midnight knew that he was not the big chief of this tribe, because right now the big chief was lying on his belly with a Derringer pointing into his face. Midnight had had to kill a man — a lone Indian sentry — in order to get his 'insurance' a policy that he hoped to redeem some time that morning.

The chief had white stripes radiating from his hooked nose, and there was red rouged into the hollows of his eyes which gave him a diseased and repulsive appearance. He wore nothing on his body save a loin cloth. In his deerskin belt was a tomahawk, and that was the only weapon the chief carried, though his men had plenty of rifles. He was a brave if savage man, this Penateka chief.

Midnight gave the customary greeting. 'How, red brother.'

And the chief said, 'How, white man.'

Midnight took his time, then said, easily, 'What does my red brother want, following our tracks so early in the morning?'

A gleam came to those black eyes in their red-sore surroundings. 'Red man wantum guns. Heap plenty guns white man got. Red man say, give guns, red man no hurt white man.'

Midnight didn't understand, though he thought he did. He laughed sardonically. 'Like hell we'll give you our guns, Injun. Jes' you think o' somethin' else funny, yeah?' If they surrendered their arms to these Indians he didn't give much for the promise that they would be allowed to go unscathed.

So, thought Midnight sardonically, these Injuns had as much chance of getting his weapons in surrender as he had of biting his way through these hills.

But the next words of the Indian's startled him. The chief grunted. 'White man him got plenty guns to fight damn' *yanquis*. We do big trade, huh?'

Midnight's eyes narrowed. It was evident, for some incomprehensible reason, these Indians thought that his wagons were loaded with guns. He didn't deny it — if that gave further valuable minutes of time, okay, they could go on thinking they had guns.

He said, 'Why should red man think

paleface has guns?'

The chief answered shrewdly, 'Why should paleface use old soldiers' road when better road go through cowtown on plain?' Midnight nodded. To the Indians, that must seem illogical and suspicious. Yet that wasn't sufficient to suggest they were carrying guns . . .

The chief's deep voice growled on, adding argument to argument. 'Old soldiers' road him go to Mexico, and Mexicanas buy plenty guns. Your government say no sell guns to Mexicanas, but men do it an' use back trails like you do now.' He began to get impatient. 'Enough palaver, white man. Indian want guns. If you no give, Indians got plenty guns to take yours from you.'

He was arrogant, confident in their superior strength. He waved back at his silent followers, hideous in their war-paint.

Midnight still played for time. By now, he thought, they have pulled that wagon back on the road and will be reloading it. Another quarter of an hour and the wheels should be turning again . . .

He said, slowly, 'Red man, thar ain't no guns in that train of ou'n. Jest a lot o' wire.'

'Wire?' The red man's nose wrinkled. 'Red man no savvy.'

'Wire,' said Midnight, 'is fence material to keep in a hombre's cattle. One thing, it ain't guns. We ain't got no more guns than you c'n see.'

The Indian's lip curled in scorn, and his red-rimmed eyes looked contemptuous. Deliberately he said, 'White man lie.'

Midnight's eyes narrowed coldly and with just as much deliberation he said, 'Brother, I'll have that greasy scalp o' your'n fer that.'

The chief turned and raised himself in the saddle. His right arm flung out and he shouted something in the language of the Penatekas — a language that sounded to the white man like the barking of a dog.

His hands hovered near to his guns, suspecting attack, but instead a brave detached himself from the throng and came riding forward. He was naked, save for a solitary brave's feather and a brief loin cloth. He carried a rifle slung across his shoulders, and Midnight saw that it was a latest model Winchester. The brave's face was white-daubed like his chief's.

The chief said, contemptuously, 'O Fox who has Returned, tell me again what you know to be in the white man's wagons.'

And the brave told him, and when he spoke Midnight came rearing up in his saddle, snarling in ferocious rage.

'Guns! Thar's goddamned plenty guns in them wagons,' said the brave fluently. 'Guns for the Mexes!'

'Felipe!' exclaimed Midnight, and his eyes sought under that white paint and saw that it was indeed Felipe who had been one of his followers. 'You dam' renegade!'

Almost he went for his guns, but then

he remembered the major purpose — to play for time and give the wagons chance to roll.

Haughtily the young brave said, 'I ain't no renegade, Midnight. I'm a red man, an' I've come to join my brothers. And the white man's my enemy and always has been.' His voice was passionate, and the hot blood rose within him.

Still Midnight played for time. His ears were pricked for the sound that would tell him that the wagons were on the move again. This had been a tragic hold-up.

He said, 'Reckon you did for Dandy Kiplock, then?'

For answer the renegade groped at his belt and then held up a black scalp. 'Kiplock's,' he grinned maliciously. Then he fumbled again and now both hands came up full. 'And the old Driver pair's,' he shouted exultantly. 'My first paleface scalps!'

One scalp was short and grey. The other was grey . . . but long. Like an old woman's would be.

Said Midnight, 'Felipe, you were well looked after, an' you did this. For that, Felipe, I'll hunt you down for the dog you are, blast you!'

Anger shook the renegade, and he would have come forward, only the chief barked a savage command, and Felipe slunk back into a respectful position behind the chief.

Suddenly Midnight's eyes lit up and he straightened in the saddle. He wasn't sure . . . He half turned and looked back, and King Cass slowly lifted his hand — and the thumb pointed upwards. *They* were nearer, could hear better.

The wagons were rolling again.

The Indians didn't seem to hear anything, though the noise began to grow in volume as team after team of oxen threw their weight against the yokes and dragged the groaning, protesting wagons into motion.

Midnight said, 'You know what's in them wagons, Felipe. Why're you lyin?

— an' why did you go to Devine yesterday?'

Felipe answered the second part of his question first. He was arrogant, swollen-headed with pride at his own cleverness.

'I met a man on the track. I told him where Dandy Kiplock's body was buried. He said he'd go into Devine today an' report the matter. I told him you were usin' Injuns, an' I was a tame Injun an' wouldn't stand for it.' He spat. 'The fellar said I was a good boy and gave me ten cents fer a drink.'

'You're out to stir trouble on the range?'

'We'll drive you into the sea,' boasted the youth. The chief was backing his horse, saying something. Felipe ignored him and sat his horse and shouted an insult at his former leader.

Midnight saw the slow retreat of the Indian chief and knew that the truce was rapidly coming to an end. He edged his own mount backwards. Behind him, King Cass and Joe Culloch and Mex Jacinto lifted rifles and pointed them at the chief and the renegade. Higher up the valley a forest of rifles pointed unwaveringly at Midnight. One false move and there would be three dead men in that no-man's-land between the two parties.

Midnight shouted, 'What do you want, renegade?'

And Felipe shouted back, 'Sandy Addason. An' I'll have her today!'

And Midnight saw immediately why the renegade was putting across this lie about a wagon train of guns going through the backways to Mexico. It was designed to give him the support to wipe out the train and get the girl he wanted.

And he saw now why Felipe had come from the Addason ranch — all the time he had wanted to keep close to his mistress, biding his time until an opportunity came for him to strike.

Midnight thought, 'He's sure been cunnin'. He's got us in a fine fix.' And then he snarled aloud, 'Like hell you'll get Sandy, you damn' renegade! Sandy's mine, an' no one else's gonna have her!'

Then he wheeled his horse and raced back to his men. The Indian chief barked an order to the flushed and inflated Felipe, and both cantered back to the main body of Indians. The truce was over.

As Midnight's horse came pounding up, Mex, Joe and King brought their restless, uneasy mounts under cover of an overhang at the side of the trail. It was well-timed. Midnight was on the open trail, when a single shot rang out, to be followed immediately by a ragged volley of gun-fire. Midnight was wondering if that first shot had come from the treacherous Felipe, when his horse screamed and fell forward, long neck outstretched.

Midnight's reaction was automatic. As the unfortunate beast's legs buckled, Midnight kicked his feet free of the stirrups and as the head went down between his legs he jumped.

It was perfectly timed. As his horse

rolled over with a thrashing of limbs and a high whinnying scream of pain and terror, Midnight hit the ground on both feet, and ran flat out for the overhang which screened his two companions.

Mex started to spur his horse out towards him, but Midnight bellowed, 'Back — keep under cover,' and reluctantly Mex pulled the head of his horse round and out of danger. Then Midnight came in, head first, just as the ragged volley became a torrent of screeching lead. There wasn't much skin left on his chin, but he hadn't time to notice such details.

Mex juggled his horse in closer, and Midnight staggered to his feet and grabbed a stirrup-iron. A loud drumming came to his ears, as of many unshod ponies suddenly spurring towards them. And then came the dreaded Comanche war whoops, shrill and blood-curdling and sounding like a pack of demented dogs, with their curious barking cries.

Midnight hollered, 'Git goin'. Make

fer Wee Jock an' the boys.'

Mex spurred down the steep trail, Midnight's long legs taking giant strides as he clung to the stirrup. Joe Culloch and King Cass fell in behind, going more easily. That overhang gave momentary protection, but they knew that any second now the screaming horde of savages would be racing into sight, so the pair sat round in their saddles, rifles raised and waiting.

Midnight's horse could just be seen at the bend, legs threshing in a final agony. Beyond it lay the rifle that had been jerked out of their leader's hands when he had to jump for his life.

The leading Indian came hurtling round the bend, a solitary brave, naked and with the long black forelock of his tribe streaming in the breeze. Big Joe Culloch closed one eye and squinted along his rifle barrel.

The Indian was flat along the back of his pony; suddenly he seemed to swoop and one hand reached down and with a lightning grab siezed the fallen rifle. He rose on his mount, his painted face triumphant, the rifle lifted high in the exultation of the moment.

Joe clicked his tongue, and it sounded as though he were chiding the Indian for being foolish in his action. Then his finger took first pull; a pause, then the finger squeezed . . . and the life went out of the Indian all in one second.

Then his rifle emptied with rhythmic abruptness, and the forefront of the galloping Indians went down as the bullets found easy targets in the close-packed mass of ponies. Joe galloped in, trying to reload, and now it was King Cass's turn to provide covering fire.

Lead was screaming towards them again as more Indians rounded the bend and negotiated the litter of fallen bodies on the trail. Cass deliberately wheeled his horse and faced the mass. Then his rifle crackled into spiteful hate and the spitting flame hurled lead with deadly effect into the throng.

Cass kicked his horse round and streaked after his companions. Round another bend he ran past a stolid, baccychewin' Joe Culloch, who had reloaded and was prepared to take up the fight.

It gave Mex and Midnight a chance and they took it. Afterwards Midnight swore that the soles of his boots grew so hot they made permanent footprints on the rocky trail. Wee Jock, Skippy, and the Callason brothers, fretting because they could hear a fight and weren't in it, suddenly saw Mex dragging the giant-striding Midnight into view. When Midnight saw his men, he let go and staggered behind cover and then lay down for half a minute and tried to give his tortured lungs all the air they wanted. Cass rounded the bend and came riding through, then Joe Cullock came hurtling up in a manner that suggested very close pursuit.

The Indians suddenly poured into the valley. Their blood was up and they were too reckless to consider caution;

222

they never reckoned on an ambush, but that was what they ran into.

The boys lay and cuddled their rifles and didn't show a head until the Indians were well exposed to view. And then four rifles almost simultaneously crackled fire from positions high up on either side of the trail. Mex, Joe and King heard the roar of guns and dived off their horses — got under cover and then added their Winchesters to the slaughter.

Midnight came up with his Colts then, but they were useless at that range, so he knelt and watched the Indians go down like weeds before a sickle. After a while it became difficult to hit an Indian because of the confused pile of bodies, men's and ponies', that sprawled across the track. Midnight, closest to the Indians, saw them pull away and run for cover. He tried to estimate how many there were left mounted, and thought there could still be twenty or thirty. Then he saw fleet-footed braves coming into sight at the end of the valley, and knew that the next phase of the battle was to begin.

For a time hostilities ceased as the Indians carefully surveyed the situation from behind a rock barrier where the trail left this rugged valley. Midnight saw the bobbing feathered head-dresses of the chiefs, and divined what would come next.

He crawled on his belly to where Mex, Joe and King lay at the side of the trail. Joe was rolling a cigarette and complained when he found it nipped smartly out of his fingers and put into Midnight's grinning mouth. Midnight said, 'I c'd do with a smoke after that run, Joe,' so Joe rolled himself another cigarette.

They lay for ten minutes with the sun burning their backs and sending the air up in shimmering waves from the blisteringly hot rocks around them.

Midnight said, 'I guess this defence of our'n will make 'em feel sure I lied when I said we didn't carry no guns in the wagons.' He told of his pow-wow with the chief and the renegade, while they watched the wounded Indians crawl painfully back to cover.

King Cass swore, 'I'll get that varmint, Felipe. I never did like the breed. Guess he thought too much of hissel' ter be any good.'

Felipe was in for a rough time of it, if ever he were caught; only Midnight, watching a shadow, wasn't so sure if he would ever be caught — by them.

For that shadow was moving, and incredibly it was in a position almost directly above them — just where Wee Jock McCraw lay with his rifle that was nearly his own height.

Midnight reached out without looking, took King Cass's rifle and levelled it. When the shadow moved again he squeezed the trigger, and a brave silently stepped out into thin air, and just as silently fell eighty feet until his body broke on the rocky valley bottom.

Wee Jock was round on his knee and blazing upwards. These Indians had been slicker than they'd guessed. The dismounted braves had immediately been sent up into the hills to get above and behind them, and they had nearly succeeded. Midnight guessed they must have found some hidden trail up there among the rocky spurs and pinnacles.

He saw more movements, and now they seemed to come at regular intervals. A lot of braves were up there and now a few began to shoot down at them.

Midnight cupped his hands to his mouth and shouted a warning. 'Pull out, Fred — Jock. It'll be too hot in a minute. Get your hosses — now!'

The rifle fire from above quickened as the Callason brothers, Wee Jock and Skippy suddenly leapt from cover and raced to their mounts. In the valley bottom Midnight and his three companions blazed away, first with rifles and then with Colts in an effort to give cover to their companions.

Midnight saw his followers leap into their saddles and come spurring down, to converge on the trail. Then he saw

Wee Jock straighten in agony, and then slowly slump across the neck of his frightened mount.

Big Tom Midnight came to his feet at once, holstering his guns, and shouting, 'Jock's hit. Come a-runnin'!'

Then Wee Jock's terrified horse came bolting towards him, neck outstretched, eyes rolling and showing the whites, mouth opened in a thin scream of terror as the roar of guns echoed and re-echoed along the valley bottom.

Midnight timed his jump beautifully. One minute the horse was travelling by with a solitary swaying huddle of a figure in the saddle; the next two were up, as Midnight grabbed a handful of mane and in the same instant swung lightly on to the horse's bare rump.

The big cowboy grabbed for leather, found it clutched in Wee Jock's fading grip, and fought for control. Behind him came his followers.

And behind them, screaming their victory whoops again, streamed the mounted Comanches.

Within yards the strong hands of the cowboy had the horse under control again. Wee Jock's dwarfish face came round slowly, to grin weakly and whisper, 'Good boy, Tom . . . '

He was bady hurt and needed attention urgently, but there was no time to look after him now. Too many lives were at stake for that, and Wee Jock knew it.

Midnight gasped, 'Stick it out, Jock. We've still got to put up a delayin' action. Guess them wagons ain't more'n a mile or so down the trail yet.'

They played at leap-frog for the next five minutes. Mex, Joe and King Cass stood across the trail and pumped lead into the howling Indians and drove them back into cover. Then, with their guns empty, they wheeled and raced down the stony track, while the Callason brothers, Skippy Playfellow and Midnight reined round and emptied their rifles into the screaming, maddened beasts and men — Midnight using Wee Jock's which had stuck in the boot during the scramble on to the main trail back there.

Each time the groups of cowboys turned, the Indians would dive for cover. But they were getting wise to the tactics, and Midnight saw that the Indians were gaining on them. More, they were beginning to use their rifles more coolly, and at this range even their out-of-date weapons would soon find targets.

Then it seemed that they ran into disaster again.

Midnight and his two comrades came wheeling round a bend, and the cowboy saw someone sitting a horse before him. He had forgotten . . . it was Sandy, waiting for him.

But — and this was the disaster — just behind the girl and blocking the track, was the last of the wagons. The wagons that should have been a mile or two along the trail by now.

14

Sweating, Midnight pulled his horse back on to its haunches. A hundred yards to the rear, Mex, Joe and King Cass suddenly opened up a withering volley of fire that would check the Indians for a half minute or so.

Midnight called, 'Sandy — what happened?' He saw that bundle across the front of her saddle stir at sound of his voice.

She wheeled her horse round to face the wagon. Men were working frantically at it, easing it round a narrow part of the trail. Sandy shouted, 'A wheel on the second wagon hit a rock and started a slide that half covered the track. We had to stop and clear it; then it's been tricky, manoeuvring the wagons round it with only that narrow space to work in.'

Midnight said, 'Take this hoss,

Sandy; I'll use your'n. An' get Wee Jock into one o' the wagons. I reckon the li'l runt's hit bad.'

Sandy slid down, while Midnight vaulted off his horse. He hoisted her up into the saddle, then banged the horse and sent it flying away down the trail, just as a cheer from the struggling teamsters told him that the last wagon was through.

He looked round. This wasn't a bad place for a stand.

He called across to the panting Callason brothers and Skippy Playfellow — 'Get behind that fall of rock, an' cover me with your rifles. I'm gonna cash in on that insurance policy I took out last night.'

He was stripping the blanket off the bundle before him as he spoke. The Indian chief's head snaked round in venomous hate as the blanket was tossed aside. Big Tom Midnight released the gag from the chief's mouth and rapped, 'You wanta live after today?' The chief licked dry lips but said nothing. Midnight continued grimly, 'Well, I guess it ain't in your hands. Guess it's up to your pals, not you.'

Mex Jacinto came belting into sight then, to be followed by Joe Culloch and King Cass. They started to pull up at sight of Midnight trotting towards them, but he waved them on and shouted, 'Get behind them rocks!'

They rode on and flung themselves behind the pile of boulders that had fallen on to the trail, just as the first Indians came swooping round the bend. They saw Midnight appear to be engulfed by the horde; one moment he was there alone on the trail — the next he was surrounded by excited, shrilling Indians.

Then they saw the Indians part, and Midnight came calmly backing his horse out of the ruck, and it didn't make sense to them for a minute. Those Indians were actually falling back.

Fred Callason said, 'That sure is a powerful insurance that old Tom took out last night. Guess I must do business with that company sometime.'

It took them a while to see that Midnight had hoisted the Indian chief across the horse before him. The chief's hands were still behind his back, and he was helpless with Big Tom's powerful hands clasped around his neck. And to make things more awkward, one of Midnight's big blue Colts was pressing hard into the side of his head.

That was what had sent the Indians withdrawing from their paleface enemy. They could see that before they took him he would dispatch their chief to the Happy Hunting Grounds from which not even brave chieftains can return.

He was a brave chief. He sat, stony-faced and apparently unmindful of the threat to his life, and he never cried out once — never once shouted to his men to keep back or they would cost him his life.

Probably it was because he was such a brave man that his followers didn't press forward, didn't want to see him killed.

So they stood back and talked, and every second that passed gave the wagons opportunity to widen the distance between them. Sitting there with the brown, naked body in front of his own, almost as brown, just as naked body, Midnight tried to reckon how many more miles those wagons had to go before coming within the safety of the Ricketts' holdings. He calculated nine miles. That was four hours' travelling, with oxen and wagons laden as heavily as theirs, and only four hours if they drove the teams unmercifully.

He sighed. Four hours was a lot of time to buy.

Then he saw a movement to get around him on the part of some unmounted Indians. He kneed his horse rearwards a few more steps and outwitted the move, then sat and calmly waited for more time to pass.

Suddenly he began to hear Felipe's voice, and at once the second Colt leapt into his left hand. If Felipe showed his face for an instant a heavy .45 bullet would smash into his skull and end his double-dealing life.

But Felipe kept hidden among the Indians. Maybe he was a wise renegade and knew what to expect if he showed himself.

One of the chiefs stepped forward. He was a young man and might have been the captive's son. He spoke in that queer barking language of the Penatekas, addressing the chief on the horse before Midnight. But the chief made no answer, just looked over the heads of his followers back up the trail; and his eyes were filled with the disgrace that comes to a warrior who has been lifted from his bed robes and kidnapped like a child . . . His eyes said that death was the one thing he sought for now to wipe out the memory of the way he had been treated, he, a proud chief of the Penateka.

Only, Midnight didn't want him to die; not just yet. And fortunately the

Indians weren't prepared to lose a brave chief who had led them well, not for a while, anyway.

But it couldn't last.

Quarter of an hour later the Indians were arguing, discussing the position, while Midnight blocked their way with that gun to the head of the silent chief. But there was greater anger now in their voices, and their manner was momentarily growing more threatening.

Twice more, Indians cunningly tried to circle Midnight and cut him off, but each time he was too quick for them and retreated a few paces. Now he was close to the rock pile behind which his followers lay. He knew their rifles were silently covering him, and it felt good to have friends so close behind.

Another five minutes passed, and then Midnight realised that he had had almost all the value he was going to get out of his 'insurance policy.' One near-naked Indian came suddenly padding forward on moccasined feet. In his hand was a tomahawk. Midnight watched the arm go back, preparatory to throwing the weapon. He didn't wait for a shot from behind in case they couldn't see the Injun for his body. The blue Colt in his left hand barked once. The Indian threw back his head to cry out in agony, but died ere the sound came as high as his throat. He collapsed, his bare limbs jerking spasmodically in death.

And in that same second the whole mob of Indians raised a savage cry and came sweeping impulsively forward. Midnight threw his left arm lovingly round the prisoner and hid behind that bare body as guns were raised to shoot him. All the time he was steering his mount backwards into the shelter of the rock pile at the trail side.

He was level — then kicking his horse under cover.

And no one was there. He saw, for one bewildering instant, the impression made in the dust where his comrades had lain — and they no longer lay there. They had gone on without him, began a swift, enveloping thought that was the nearest thing to fear that Big Tom Midnight had ever experienced.

And then Joe Culloch's cool voice called, 'Keep a-comin' back, Tom. And — move!'

Midnight wheeled his horse and spurred back down the trail. It was a sharp turn here, where the wagons had been held up, and at the abrupt corner over-hanging the precipice, Joe Culloch and the other men were hanging on to ropes. As Midnight came up in a shower of loose stones, he saw his men kick into their horses and start them pulling on to ropes that led upwards. Twisting, he had an impression that they terminated around a projecting spur of rock, and then the projecting spur of rock was tumbling downwards, and with it came a shower of earth and boulders.

Joe Culloch roared, 'Leggo them ropes — an' beat it!'

They kicked their horses into a gallop and raced down the trail, just as the avalanche hit the narrow track. All were sitting round in their seats to watch. They saw one solitary Indian on his pony try to race across the gap. They saw what appeared to be half the mountain on the move. Then the rock slide seemed to brush the mounted Indian, and he went over the edge.

And all the way down that Indian knew he was going to his doom, and his voice floated up in a wail of horror as he went to meet the Great Spirit.

Midnight brought his horse to a walk. For the moment that trail was impassable. He said, 'That sure was a good idea, Joe.'

Joe spat complacently and said, 'Guess I hadda do somethin', the way King was a-cussin' my shootin'. When I saw that slide o' rock I thought maybe we could start another — and bigger.'

The dust was settling as the fall of earth and stone subsided. Midnight said, 'Braves afoot will be able to clamber over them rocks, but I don't reckon they'll catch us on our hosses.

It's them Injuns with their ponies we gotta fear. But they ain't gonna get over that rock pile so easy. It'll maybe take 'em an hour or so to shift it.'

King Cass caught up with him. 'You reckon they will shift it? An' keep after us?'

Midnight nodded, jogging along. 'While they think there's guns in them wagons, I don't reckon they'll ever give up the pursuit. They think we're smugglin' 'em through the territory an' won't dare run to the town for shelter. Well, they're pretty near right, only we ain't smugglin' guns; we're a-runnin' in wire in defiance o' the sheriff.'

King Cass looked at the stony-faced Indian chief sitting in front of Midnight. 'What're you gonna do with Charlie, Tom?'

Midnight considered. 'He's a damn' nuisance wearin' my hoss's strength out,' he said. Then he added, 'But the hombre's got guts, an' I ain't gonna knock him over the head like he'd knock me over mine.'

'So he c'n sit here an' wait fer his friends to come an' untie his hands,' he decided, and descending he pulled the chief to the ground. He stood him upright, then said in parting, 'It was nice knowin' you, chief. Remember me to all your squaws.'

Back he swung into the saddle, and they started to trot away. But Midnight was watching the Indian as he stood there alone on that narrow, rock-girt trail. There was something on that face that Midnight didn't like to think about. It was the face of a man who is seeing death . . .

He saw the chief stand there, very erect and very strong. And then he walked forward. Midnight shouted and pulled his horse around. But the Indian without a tremor of hesitation, took one more step forward — into space. He went down a long way, and then his body hit rocks and bounced out into space, and then hit more rocks and bounced again. And he died without a sound escaping him; and that way he hoped to atone for the disgrace that had come to him, chief of the Penatekas, of the proud tribe of Comanches.

The others had seen it happen, and Midnight sighed. 'I kinda hate to see a brave man go out like that. Guess he must have suffered hell all that time wrapped up in a blanket. Guess he knew from the beginnin' when I grabbed him in his tent that that's how it had to end.'

Joe Culloch spat, and that was the punctuation mark that ended the obituary. They turned their horses and cantered slowly down the trail together.

An hour later they came in sight of the last of the wagons. Sandy saw them and came spurring gladly back. Midnight said, 'You go ahead, Sandy; I'll only worry if we start another fight, an' I reckon it'll still come to that. Go warn old man Ricketts an' have him call his men in from around. Tell him to drive his cattle to the far end o' the range. If we lead these varmints on to his land, they'll sure try to do all the damage they can.'

Midnight's guess was good. He and the Callasans dropped back to act as rear-guard while the others went ahead to get water and a bite of food. Hardly were they in position when half a dozen mounted Indians came trotting into sight. Midnight had Wee Jock's rifle to his shoulder in an instant and shot down a couple of ponies. It was more important to kill the horses than the Indians during this pursuit.

The other Indians immediately pulled back into safety. Midnight and the Callasan brothers cautiously retreated, guns barking whenever a target showed itself. The Indians didn't seem in a hurry to mount an attack. After a while Midnight thought he understood why.

That landslide across the trail had probably been only partly cleared, and under the circumstances the Indians would have great difficulty in getting their horses across. Probably the rest of the mounted Indians were strung down the trail, catching up with the first across the blocked trail.

'Waal, I reckon that gives us a bit more time,' he drawled to Rob Calla-san. And time was precious. The trail was nowhere near as steep now, and the going was a lot easier. Against that the oxen were almost dropping with fatigue, and it seemed unlikely they would last out for the hour or so that was still needed to bring them out of the foothills.

And then? Maybe they'd be in even worse position, with a couple of miles of open prairie to cross, and these heathens able to ride swiftly up and encircle the slow, lumbering wagons.

But the future could take care of itself. He fired a speculative shot at an incautious brave and saw rock splinters go up into the fierce bronzed face and heard a howl float down the trail to him.

The rest of the boys came up at a gallop then. Joe Culloch said that Wee Jock was very ill but he guessed he'd be all right if he could soon be got out of that jolting, uncomfortable wagon. Joe spoke with difficulty. There was a large hunk of meat in his mouth, and a larger piece still in his hand. He suddenly fired one-handed, the Winchester held to his side. An Indian fell off his pony and went crawling away, one leg dragging.

So time went on, and all the time the trail became easier and not so abrupt in descent, and the valley was widening and the hills on either side grew less steep and easier to negotiate.

And behind them the Indians massed, biding their time now until they were in overwhelming force and with easier ground on which to start their attack.

It came almost the moment that the leading wagon left the hills and ran out on to the prairie — Ricketts' land. Here the valley widened until it was half a mile across — and widened still more with every yard. Suddenly, at a signal from their chief, two lines of mounted Indians shot out in a clear attempt to encircle the wagon train.

Midnight looked forward across the wide, almost boundless prairie. Ahead of him he could see the buildings of the Ricketts' place, lying against a background of scrub-covered hills. He was thinking that in those hills lay a scalped body, when a stir of dust far down the trail took his eye.

Someone was coming out fast to meet them.

He shouted encouragement to his men, then rode close up alongside the wagons. The Indians drew level, then started to swoop in to meet each other across the prairie trail. Midnight got the range, fired, and horse and naked rider went somersaulting into the sage brush. The rest of his men started shooting now, and the fire was so devastating that the Indians sheered off for the moment and went galloping parallel to the wagons.

But they were all firing into the train now, and beginning to close in. There seemed as many Indians now as when the attack started that morning, and more were streaming down the valley trail behind them. It was evident that the insurrection up at Wichita was attracting big reinforcements from all over Texas — it was an Indian uprising on a big scale.

The oxen were pulling weakly now. At the rate they were travelling, Midnight knew they would never last the remaining distance to the protection of the Ricketts' ranch. But there was nothing they could do, except flog them and keep them going, and hope somehow they would win victory over the Indians with their last gasp.

Whips cracking, men's hoarse voices bellowing, axles screeching and the heavy, laden timbers groaning, the cavalcade crawled slowly across the prairie. Then the Indians came wheeling in a sudden savage charge. Guns grew hot as they were emptied rapidly, and the Colts leapt out as the nearly naked, screaming Indians came riding right in amongst the wagons.

And then someone else came riding in among the train. Sandy and a dozen of Ricketts' men. Reinforcements!

The shock hurled the Indians back. For a moment they probably imagined it to be a greater reinforcement than it actually was. They pulled their horses round and instinctively rode wide so as to get out of range of the deadly guns, and by the time they had collected their wits, a determined cordon of nineteen men and a girl was riding round those wagons.

After a few minutes they came charging in again, their war whoops hideous to hear. But they had lost too many men now to be effective, and when that blistering fire came at them, except in one place they all turned and rode quickly back into the hills.

That one place was right by where Sandy was riding. She was using a Colt which she must have picked up at the ranch, and as half a dozen yelling braves rode in at her she began to fire, but her aim wasn't so good.

Midnight pulled his horse round and went streaking in to the rescue. He saw the Indians milling around the girl, and then she was pulled off her mount and they began to ride away in a triumphant little body.

And then Midnight was in upon them. He came in so quickly that they were taken unawares; and he did the only thing possible against their superior numbers.

He took a flying leap out of his saddle, and swept both Sandy and her captor with a crash to the ground. His own hands gripped the throat of the redskin while they were still in mid-air, continued to grip as they reached the ground, and never stopped gripping until there wasn't a movement left in the brave.

Midnight saw Sandy start to life herself and shouted, 'Keep down, Sandy. Don't lift your head.' Because he knew what the boys would do. Lead zipped past and tore into the braves who had captured the girl. They had turned, determined to recapture the girl, but when the rifles opened up they changed their minds and raced swiftly away after their fellows.

When the firing had ended, Midnight rolled the dead Indian over so that he could see through the paint on his face. He was disappointed. He had half-expected this to be Felipe, but evidently Felipe didn't come up so closely with the attack.

He went over to Sandy. She was in pain, and pretty white about the face. 'Honey,' he whispered, 'I gotta get outa this habit of knockin' you off horses, else there won't be no gal for me to marry.'

His arms went under her and lifted. She settled into them with a sigh. Whispered, 'I don't care how often it happens, so long as I always finish up in your arms.'

Next moment they were surrounded by milling horses, and willing offers were made to give them a lift.

And so, with the sun still high in the

sky, the weary train crept the last half-mile to where old man Ricketts stood, rifle in his gnarled, ageing hand. Within the shelter of the buildings, the oxen collapsed to their knees while water was brought for them, and the teamsters, Midnight and his men just lay in the shade and recovered from their race against death.

But it was a happy band of men — and one rather bruised girl — who sat down to the meal that was prepared an hour late. A cold sluice and a fresh shirt did wonders — the food and drink finished the miracle off. As Skippy Playfellow remarked, 'Doggone, now I guess I got strength enough to lie down an' sleep fer a fortnight.'

But Midnight, suddenly rising, wanting sleep himself, had seen a movement down the range. It came from a place near to where the fence had been bust that night not long ago. He watched. There was nothing he could do about this. But when he had opportunity he went over to Ricketts and said, 'We just get out o' one lot o' trouble an', geewillikins, here comes some more!'

Old Ricketts lifted his bushy eyebrows. 'I don't *sabe?*' So Midnight sat down and told him. 'Tomorrow,' he prophesied, 'there'll be a coupla hundred armed men a-ridin' in from Devine. They'll come with ropes, an' I guess there'll be one fer my neck fer certain, an' maybe they'll have some to fit the rest o' my boys. Don't reckon they'll do much more than knock you about a bit fer bein' a fencer,' he added kindly.

Ricketts said, 'That feels kinda reassuring. Now you tell me why you're so certain 'bout this.'

Midnight sighed. 'Felipe went an' told someone where to find Dandy Kiplock's body. The fellar said he'd go to town today and tell somebody what he'd been told. Reckon some guys have just got around to testing the truth of what had been told 'em.'

'You mean — ?'

'Sure.' Midnight nodded. 'There's a

passel o' men right by where we buried Dandy. Reckon he's dug up now an' across someone's hoss on his way fer Paul Kiplock to see him. An' when Paul sees that scalping — '

Old man Ricketts sighed and went across for the gun he had so lately put down. 'Looks like this time I'm gonna need this,' he said. And then he whistled. 'Two hundred white men. Guess that's some proposition. Now, Injuns, I could scare that number myself!'

15

They got the teamsters and their wagons away at dawn, because Midnight didn't want them around if there was trouble. They watched the weary cavalcade as it climbed back of them over the hills towards Devine, and then Midnight turned to Ricketts and said, 'Reckon you'd better call your men an' tell 'em we might have to stand siege. Maybe some won't want to go so far agen the fence busters ef they know about the scalpin'.'

Ricketts walked over to the men's bunkhouse and put the situation to them. He needed all the men he could keep, but it was no use talking men into staying if their hearts weren't in it. He told the silent, listening punchers about Felipe and the scalped man.

'You know how I feel about fencing,' he ended gruffly. 'The old days of free range are over, an' we might as well get used to the idea. I guess that if we make a stand an' show the country that fence bustin' ain't no proposition, half the ranchers hereabouts will come flocking fer wire. But — first we've got to make a stand, an' they're gonna be rough because of that blamed renegade a-goin' an' a-scalpin' Dandy Kiplock. Ef you don't want to stay, better pack your traps an' git.'

The men conferred together. Then a couple went across and started packing. The foreman, a young fellow from a northern state, stepped forward and said, 'We don't all reckon to share your views on fencin', boss, but you've always been a straight-shooter with us, so we reckon to stand by you now.'

Old man Ricketts nodded and stumped back to where Midnight was sitting astride the veranda rail and watching back along the trail to Devine. 'All told, includin' your men, Tom, we got twenty-three, an' that includes you an' me.'

Sandy came out with some coffee. 'Make it twenty-four and add my Derringer to the total. What do you think I'm going to do if there's a fight starts up? Sit around and swoon?'

Big Tom Midnight slipped his arm round her and grinned. 'You're a hell-cat, honey, but that's the kinda gal we need in Texas.' Then he said, with another smile, 'There's Wee Jock in there who won't let me take his guns from his bedside. I guess we c'n count on a twenty-fifth man ef it comes to close work.'

He stopped abruptly, his eyes narrowing to take in the far distant swirl of dust that spoke of approaching riders. 'Here it comes,' he said softly, 'What I've been expectin' . . .'

Sheriff Con Tierney was leading the party, and he was red-faced and sweating from the hot, dusty journey, and bad-tempered because of the unaccustomed exercise. Behind him rode Paul Kiplock, his thin face dark and full of fury. And with this pair were half a dozen citizens of Devine, pressed into service as sheriff's deputies.

Tierney didn't dismount. He looked down, his eyes resting on Midnight, and spoke harshly. 'Paul Kiplock an' some of his men came yesterday an' found the body of Dandy Kiplock just off the Ricketts' land. Dandy had died from knifing in the back, and then he'd been scalped. We got information that it was one of your imported gunnies that did it, Midnight, so I'm holdin' you responsible. I'm gonna take you back to town to await trial, an' I aim to take your gunnies with you.'

Midnight said, easily, 'Sure I'll go back to Devine with you, Tierney — when I'm tired o' life.' His manner changed to contempt, 'What the hell, Tierney, do you think I was born yesterday? You know I'd never get as far as your office — the mob would come an' string me up an' my buddies, too. An' you wouldn't stop 'em, would you?'

Tierney rapped, 'It's my duty to take you in, Midnight. You're the cause of all this bother on the range, an' I aim to stop it — now. You'll get a fair trial.'

Midnight said, 'I ain't comin', Tierney. Now what're you gonna do?'

Tierney's eyes flickered over the cowboys lounging against the corral rails. They appeared indolent and at ease, but he wasn't deceived. He knew that one false move and six or seven pairs of hands would be streaking for guns.

The sheriff said, 'Ef you won't come of your own free will, Midnight, I reckon I'll have to get a big enough posse to take you, that's all. An' ef Ricketts harbours you, he'll have to stand the consequences.'

Ricketts spat. 'Guess I bin doin' that for nigh on seventy year. I ain't skeered o' your threats, Tierney. I won't turn any friend o' mine in.'

Tierney nooded broodingly. 'That's as it may be. There ain't nothin' left fer me but to raise the countryside agen you.' He pulled round, ready for the long ride back to town.

Midnight said, softly, 'An' that's what everythin's about, ain't it, Tierney? Raisin' the countryside — startin' a range war. It's why you took pay from them blamed Easterners, ain't it? Only it looks like this scalpin' has made things a bit one-sided for the moment. When we're gone you'll have to start all over agen, makin' trouble.'

Tierney's face came round, black and snarling. 'By God, Midnight, you'll regret that,' he was saying, and it was just at that second that Paul Kiplock's horse jumped forward — and Midnight found himself with a gun pressing into his cheek, and Paul's savage, exultant face peering down at him from the saddle.

Paul shouted, 'Don't none of you make a move, else I'll blow this varmint to kingdom come.' He slipped down from his horse, that gun muzzle never moving from Midnight's face. 'You thought you could defy us, uh? But I warn't goin' with you, you devil you!' It almost looked as though he would pull the trigger at that moment, and Sandy came forward, her hands to her mouth to hold back the exclamation of horror.

Only Midnight didn't seem over-perturbed. He said, 'Don't be a fool, Kiplock. I never killed your brother, an' the fellow who did is a renegade an' I'm gonna kill him myself. He scalped the old Driver pair, an' he told where he had hid Dandy's body, only he's thrown the blame on to me and these other men o' mine. Guess he told a powerful nasty tale agen us, too.'

Paul Kiplock said, 'That makes no odds, Midnight. You started all this — '

Midnight said dryly, 'It could be argued that the fence busters started everythin'.'

Then Midnight said, casually, 'Guess I'm tired o' that gun pressin' into my head, Paul. Guess it kinda feels unfriendly . . . ' In the middle of a sentence he dropped flat to the ground.

One shot instantly rang out from behind them, and Paul Kiplock jumped back in pain as his revolver went jerking from his hand.

Sandy wheeled. A small, dwarfish face grinned from over a window-sill, back of a Winchester. And Wee Jock drawled, complacently, 'You knew you could depend on me, Tom, didn't you?' Then his voice went steel-hard. 'Git on your hoss, hombre, an' then the whole blamed lot o' you git to hell outa here. I'm a sick man, an' I don't reckon to git myself excited unduly.'

Midnight's men detached themselves from the fence and ambled towards the mounted posse. No one had seen it happen, but somehow guns had appeared in all their hands Big Joe Cullock said, mildly, 'Reckon you'd better do as Wee Jock says. He gets all-fired mean, that li'l runt.'

Tierney snarled, 'Okay — but we'll be back with more guns than you've got.'

Then they whirled and went pounding back up the trail.

* * *

Skippy Playfellow sounded the warning an hour or so after noon. He'd been riding the fence, and he came loping up to the corral where Ricketts was waiting.

He sat his saddle and rolled a cigarette, drawling comfortably, 'Guess you oughta say goodbye to your fence, old-timer.'

Ricketts looked round. 'They comin'?'

Skippy struck a match on his tight-stretched pants. 'They sure are. They're sneaking down a wooded gully back along the fence apiece. Guess they don't know I saw 'em.'

'How many?' — Midnight.

'Dozens . . . maybe hundreds. I couldn't see all that good. Some have got axes, an' I reckon they aim to tear up the fences as a start.'

They went back to the house, which was built up a piece. There was no sign of the fence busters, but it wasn't hard to imagine where they were and what they were doing, from what Skippy had told them.

Ricketts pointed to where the fence

sank out of sight along the sunken trail that parelleled the brush country and the low hills. 'There's a couple o' miles of fence down that draw,' he said. 'Guess they'll work their way along it, an' then come an' talk with their guns agen us.'

Sandy caught Midnight out on the back porch. She put her hands on his shoulders and said, 'Tom, I think you should take horse and get out of the state. That scalping's turned the countryside against you, and I don't reckon you have a chance now. Go, darling — I'll follow later.'

Midnight slipped his arms round her. He didn't seem a worried man at all. 'If I run out, honey, it'll always be held against me, that even if I didn't do it myself I caused Dandy Kiplock to be scalped. I'll be a fugitive on the run for ever, an' that ain't no life for a man who's got his mind set on marryin'.'

He smiled down. 'Besides, honey, if I run out, it leaves Ricketts an' his men to face up to a mighty unpleasant mob.'

His eyes came lowering down through the curly mesquite. An Indian sat there looking at him. Midnight saw a fierce brown face with white daub makings in the shadows of the brush. His eyes went travelling swiftly aound and across the mesquite. Then he turned the girl and slowly walked her inside the house.

And then he deserted her, and she thought he had gone mad.

He raced first to one window and then to another, and then he went hurtling out into the sunshine and pounded across to where the boys were standing looking out to see where the fence busters would be at work.

She saw men suddenly galvanised into action. In one second the entire ranch became a hubbub of feverish activity. Men came hurtling into the house, fixing up shutters and laying out cases of ammunition. Others went and lay down alongside the corrals and by the barns. And she noticed that no longer was their attention directed all to one spot — the sunken trail where the fence was — but it seemed to be everywhere all around them.

Instinctively she got hold of the Colt she had borrowed the previous day from old man Ricketts, then she ran across to where a sweating Joe Culloch was carrying a mighty pile of shutters along the veranda.

She called, 'Joe, what is it? What's happened? Has everyone gone crazy?'

Joe dropped the load and spoke, but he went on working frantically at boarding up the house. 'We gone crazy,' he gasped. 'Guess we forgot one important thing. Take a look — anywhere you like.'

She ran to the rail and looked. There were Indians staring at her from the mesquite only a hundred yards or so away. She looked north, to where the back trail went over the hills to Devine. And there was a line of silent menacing red men lurking in the bush. Then she looked south and saw a massed party of mounted Indians trotting across the prairie, and there must have been a hundred to a hundred and fifty of these alone.

'Good heavens,' gasped Sandy. 'There must be hundreds of them. But — why?'

Joe was making a good job of things. Every shutter was being nailed up. He called across, 'They must have called up reinforcements in the night. An' why? They got an uprising way north at Wichita, and when you're revoltin' agen the white man what's more valuable than gold but guns?'

'Guns?' Sandy began to understand.

'Yeah, guns. They still think we've got an arsenal of guns hid up at this place, an' they reckon to get 'em for their own use. Guess they think they've only a handful of palefaces agen their hundreds. Guess — '

Sandy never knew what further guess big Joe Culloch was going to make. She had turned at the sound of a horse suddenly jumping into a gallop away from the ranch buildings. Then a cry of horror and bewilderment rose from her.

Heading south, almost directly for

the mounted party of Indians, was a lone puncher.

Midnight.

He was flat across the back of his horse, spurring it into its fastest pace. Then she caught the gleam of something bright in his hand, and knew he was riding with his Colt out, ready for action.

Mex Jacinto came running across on stiff, bow legs. 'Tom says you're to get back into the house an' stay inside at all costs,' he shouted, then came running up the steps. 'Joe, you'n me's gotta stay near Sandy an' not let her outa sight for a minute — Boss's orders. He reckons that Felipe's saddled hisself with this lie that we're holdin' guns, an' he reckons he'll desert his new pals afore they find out he's bin lying to them. But afore he does that, Midnight reckons he'll try an' grab Sandy — he's crazy enough fer anythin'!'

Sandy wanted to stay outside and watch, but just at that moment a solitary rifle cracked off, and they knew that the fight against the horde of Indians had begun. They hustled her into cover, so that she didn't see what happened to Midnight.

He had been giving orders for the defence of the ranch, and was watching that slow-moving band of mounted red-skins, when suddenly he divined their purpose.

One of their scouts must have spotted the fence busters working along that sunken trail; now they were riding up, ready to charge down on the unprepared white men and wipe them out.

A horse was standing near by, ready saddled — it was probably Skippy Playfellow's. Midnight roared, 'I'm goin' to warn the fence busters. Guard the ranch — an' you, Mex, you an' Joe keep watch over Sandy. Felipe'll try'n get her.' Then he hurled himself on to the startled horse and went streaking off across the prairie.

At first he rode straight for the Indians. If he had headed for the sunken trail they would have guessed his intention and would have spurred their mounts into a gallop that would have beaten him to his target.

As it was they reined, halting at sight of one lone white man racing straight up towards them. They were momentarily foxed, as Midnight had hoped they would be.

Then, fifty yards from the Indians, Midnight, swerved almost obliquely away and headed for the trail. In an instant they were after him, and he heard the unshod hooves of the Indians' ponies as they drummed in pursuit.

But his lead was good enough. When he knew that the sound of firing would be heard by anyone down the gulch he started to fire back at the leading Indians. He didn't do much damage at that range, against fast-moving targets, with short-range Colts, but he had the satisfaction of seeing one pony go down and one Indian ride suddenly out to the flank, gripping a bloody wound in his stomach.

Midnight came galloping up the trail . . . and the fence busters weren't there, and the barbed wire fence still stood. There was only one thing for it — hope he hadn't been mistaken in supposing that the fence busters *were* somewhere along this fence line, and keep moving towards them. If they weren't there — He shrugged.

He sent his horse sliding on its haunches down the stony slope into the sunken trail, then swerved along it, with the new barbed wire fence that had cost so much in life and labour close by between him and the scrub-covered hill country beyond.

Round the next bend he ran full tilt into the fence busters.

They had been eating their way along that fence, chopping the wire into useless lengths and uprooting the posts. By now they had probably destroyed the better part of two miles of fencing.

And there seemed to be hundreds of them at first sight, though in a moment Midnight was to wish there was that number. He guessed there must have been a hundred or more, anyway.

They had stopped working momentarily at the sound of his guns, but it was clear they had never expected an attack from a horde of Indians. They had their faces turned towards him as he came spurring frantically round the trail and into view; and when they recognised him an exultant yell went up and they dropped cutters and axes and started to rush towards him.

'Get back,' roared Midnight. 'Indians! Get your guns!'

Then the first of the mounted Indians showed their long black forelocks and feathered head-dresses above the edge of the high ground to the west of them. A gasp rose from the fence busters. Here was a savage, formidable foe — and in a majority. More, they had an advantage.

For many of the fence busters had come with no others arms than the axes they carried, and yet others had stacked their rifles away while they worked.

Now these latter started to run towards their weapons, but in that same moment the whole line of Indians came swarming to the edge of the bluff, leaping their horses into space, so that there was a vivid instant of bronzed Indian flesh, swarthy savage faces bedaubed with war paint, dyed feathered headdresses and many-coloured ponies silhouetted against the intense blue of the Texas sky.

They came over in a mighty wave that seemed irresistible, screaming their wild war whoops, their ponies adding terrified cries to the din. The white men, all except Midnight on foot, broke and ran hard down the trail.

Midnight's guns belched into flame as he sought to give protection to the running men, but many were immediately overtaken and then the tomahawks rose and fell in a savagery of hacking, and then the scalping knives came out.

But down the line the rest of the men

had had warning, and now they swung into their saddles and came in a swift charge to where their comrade fence busters ran afoot towards their mounts.

There was a moment of impact, as horse smashed into Indian pony, and then white man and red man were locked in vicious hand to hand fighting. For a few moments the sunken road was a river of fighting men, and the noise of shouting and shooting, and blood-lusting Indian war whooping was bedlam.

And then the Indians seemed to melt back and recede as the superior fire-power of the white man's close-quarters' weapons took savage toll — against the deadly six-gun, the toma-hawk and hunting-knife were almost useless.

Suddenly those men who had been running for their horses got to them, swung up and immediately hurled their weight into the battle ... and turned it.

Suddenly the Indians were all streaming up the side of the sunken road, sometimes toppling backwards where the going was too rough or too steep, and then they were galloping away on to the prairie, to the protection of that larger force of foot warriors who were charging in on the ranch defenders.

The Indians weren't by any means defeated yet.

White men down the sunken road shouted to each other to hold up and not set off in reckless pursuit; seasoned Indian fighters, they knew better than to be lured by the foxy Indian out of their compact fighting mass.

At once the white men formed up, so that they could see what casualties they had sustained and what manner of defence or offence their strength offered against their wild enemy.

And Midnight came riding into their midst, all personal danger forgotten.

Suddenly there was a smashing blow to the side of his head, and slowly his long, lean body toppled out of the saddle and on to the dust. He lay still, blood trickling from the close dark hair on his skull.

16

Midnight stirred and came back to consciousness as rough hands dragged him to his feet. He shook his head and it began to clear. All he could remember was that he had been struck down by a treacherous blow.

Someone was shouting. He saw a thin-faced, dark hombre with a pair of fancy shooting-irons in his belt. Sight of those ornamented guns, so easy to describe, jerked Midnight's head back.

The hombre was shouting, 'Goddam you, Midnight! You bring them Injuns down to attack us when we was taken unaware. Goddam you fer a renegade white man, a-scalpin' people!'

His hand came swinging round and the fancy rings on his fingers cut open Midnight's mouth and he tasted blood. Somewhere in the crowd someone shouted, 'Hold hard there, Gun. That guy didn't look like no friend o' them pesky Injuns to me. Reckon he looked like someone doin' 'em a lot o' damage.'

Midnight got his mouth open. Three or four men were holding him tightly. One was his old friend the Longhorn, and the leer on his big, hairy face wasn't good to see.

Midnight shouted, 'You darn fools, I came to warn you. Them Injuns was a-sneakin' up on you, so I came beltin' out or they'd have caught you with your pants down.'

The thin-faced man shouted quickly, 'He's a lyin' varmint. He came for him, let's string him up.'

Then a man came pushing through to the front of the crowd, and there was a brace of Colts in his hands. He snapped, 'Listen to that firin', you damn' fool. We ain't got time to argy over a fencer while there's white men fightin' it out with Injuns.'

Midnight tried to pull himself free, but his captors hadn't released their hold on him. So he shouted, 'He's right. There's four or five hundred Injuns out there, an' only a couple dozen men at the Ricketts' ranch, an' a place the size of a town to hold. We gotta get through to help 'em, that's our first job.'

This time he was looking round for authority in the shape of the sheriff, but for once he wasn't to be seen. Midnight wondered if he were coming in with an official posse along the back trail; if so he was going to run slap into a horde of Indians.

The Longhorn now spoke, his voice a roar. 'The hell, I ain't gonna risk my skin for the sake o' some blamed fencers. They c'n fight it out themselves. I vote fer pullin' out an' letting the redskins do our work for us, an' we'll settle fer this scalpin' varmint while they do it.'

It was a cunning move, but the Longhorn didn't reckon for the fact that most men there, even though they were lawless fence busters, were otherwise good citizens. And the law of the

West was that white men always stood together in the face of the common enemy, the red man.

That man who had come through the crowd with guns ready spoke again. And now his guns were lifting. 'Gun De Leon,' he rapped, 'I'm agen fencin' myself, only I'm agen it for personal reasons, *and not because someone's paid me to be agen it*. An' I'm still a man for justice, an' I ain't gonna see no one lynched by New York-bought trouble-makers like you.'

Midnight said, 'I allus reckoned you were a fair man, Ben Coe.' Then he looked into the other man's face and said, 'You're Gun De Leon. I've sworn to kill you, an' by God I'm gonna do it.'

And then he understood why De Leon was in such an all-fired hurry to get him strung up. He, Midnight, had twice sent a message through to De Leon, telling him he was a-gunning for him and aimed to get him. De Leon daren't let him free now, because he knew that Midnight would catch up on him some day and keep his promise.

And with the crowd changing against him, *he knew he had to kill Big Tom Midnight right now*.

Midnight saw the expression on that thin, snarling dark face, saw a movement of the show-off gunman's hands towards his belt. Big Tom threw his weight into releasing his arms so that he could go for his own guns, but though he fought his way to the worn and shiny butts, those restaining hands slowed him and he was miles too late.

Only Gun De Leon never fired. Ben Coe blew the side of his head in, then stood for a second while the smoke curled up into his nostrils and De Leon's body crashed to the ground. His voice came slowly, 'I'd do that to any man that tries to shoot another held helpless.' and his eyes were a challenge to the Longhorn and his friends who were holding Midnight. There were a lot of similar-minded men in that crowd, and they showed it with growls of approval. The Longhorn snarled and relaxed his hold. Midnight stepped forward.

'Guess you did me out of one job that time, Coe,' he said slowly, looking down on the twitching limbs of the show-off gunnie. Then he looked round at the Longhorn and his friends. 'But I reckon there'll be enough shootin' to satisfy me before the day's out,' he added grimly, and climbed on to his horse. All the others were mounting.

Midnight spoke to them from his saddle, clearly. 'We don't see eye to eye over fencin', but I reckon we all look at scalpin' much the same way. It wasn't exactly one o' my men who did fer Dandy Kiplock; it was a renegade Mex-Injun from the Addason ranch who tied hisself on to us for his own reasons. He's young, and he's got the blood lust. He killed and scalped the old Driver pair — '

There was a sudden growl of anger for the men around him.

'His name's Felipe,' went on Midnight, 'and he's out there now with the

Injuns. He's the one that's caused 'em to ride out o' the hills an' make an attack on the ranch.' But he was careful not to say why.

'I'm going' back to help 'em at the ranch,' declared Midnight. 'I'll ride through singlehanded if need be — .'

Ben Coe shouted, 'The hell, take no notice o' the Longhorn, Midnight. I guess we'll all ride in with you.'

A shout went up from the men at that, and Midnight knew they would follow him . . . and suddenly realised that all in one moment he had ceased to be a prisoner of these men and instead was now their leader.

So he stood up in his stirrups and shouted, 'All right, but let's know what we're doin' afore we go chargin' in. An' when we get to the ranch we must split up, an' one half must ride to the buildings on the east side an' hold 'em, while the other half aims fer the ranch-house an' buildings on the west side. Okay?'

There was a general murmur of

understanding, and then Midnight went at a gallop down the sunken lane, keeping to cover as long as he could. And behind came well over a hundred men, leaving a dozen white men dead on the battlefield, but surrounded by at least twice their number of red men.

The big Indian attack was well under way before Midnight came hurtling in to the rescue. Inside the shuttered ranch house the gunpowder smoke filled the place with an acrid stench. Sandy was reloading and releasing jammed rounds in guns, while the rest of the ranch-house defenders picked off the red men as they came sneaking in to the attack.

When cover gave out, where the horses and cattle had trodden the ground bare, the redskins suddenly jumped to their feet with a wild whoop and came racing in to the attack. As they ran they discharged their firearms or released arrows, and then they were right up within the shelter of the sprawling buildings and smashing away at the doors and windows with their crude tomahawks.

The defenders fought back, blasting through the woodwork, first with rifles, then with heavy slugs from their deadly Colts. A door quivered under a mighty blow, and then it caved in under the sudden weight of half a dozen naked Indians wielding a wooden trough as a battering ram. Then they were fighting inside the room, and Sandy's Colt smoked twice, and then she was battering at the sweaty hands that grabbed her and started to drag her out.

And when she was outside other hands grabbed her and started to hurry off.

Then it was that Midnight came in like a wild tornado. Fifty men were close behind him, and those that weren't armed with guns had heavy axes that swung and killed every time they landed.

The fighting seemed to last for hours; in fact the Indians were routed in a matter of minutes. And once again it was the deadly Colt .45 that blasted the offensiveness out of the larger body of Indians.

Some of the buildings were blazing, where the Indians had set fire to them, and around them in the billowing smoke and fanned by the heat of the flames, men fought on horseback and afoot. Rifles barked, revolvers thundered a rolling tattoo, and men fell wounded or died, and in dying they added their cries to the hubbub of sound.

Midnight smashed his way through a struggling mass on the veranda outside the ranch-house. His guns were empty, and now they rose and fell upon the tufted, shaven scalps, as he clubbed his way to the steps.

Once there he leapt off and fought his way into the shambles of the ranch living-room. Joe Culloch was out, pretty badly hurt, but Mex and the other men were wading into the suddenly discouraged Indians.

Joe's head came up from a pool of blood on the floor. His hand pointed. 'She's gone, Tom,' he managed to shout. 'Injuns got her.'

Midnight went out, kicked an Indian in the face as he came flying up at him with a knife in his hand, and then jumped for his bucking, rearing horse and got into the saddle.

Someone was shouting to him, pointing. Midnight couldn't hear what was being said, but he guessed what was meant and spurred acoss out of the fighting. As he thundered out on to the prairie, he saw out of the corner of his eye that the white men had massed together again and were fanning out, blazing anew from reloaded four-fives and driving the Indians into retreat that would any time now become a rout.

It was the end of another sudden, savage uprising of Indians, and it had only been defeated by the coincidence of other enemies having arrived simultaneously upon the scene. But Midnight hadn't time to marvel at such pranks of coincidence.

A knot of horsemen, Indians all, were steaming out towards the hill trail, and Midnight saw someone struggling in their midst. He knew it would be Sandy and guessed that the near-naked captor would be Felipe. He had chance to slip only one round into his Colt. Midnight heard drummnig hooves behind, and looked back and saw that three or four riders were close on his heels. They scared the Indians riding companion to Sandy and her captor, and gradually they drew away from the doubly laden horse, just as Midnight raced swiftly closer to it.

Then, perhaps just at the moment when Felipe was about to drop Sandy and try to escape with his life, the breed's horse crossed its legs and went somersaulting into the mesquite.

Big Tom Midnight came swinging in with a flurry of flapping chaps. He saw Sandy rolling over and getting to her feet, and she was shouting, 'I'm all right, Tom — *watch out!'*

And Midnight made the mistake of turning and looking only towards Felipe, rising to a crouch, his face smeared where the white paint had intermingled with the blood from his fall. Brown eyes blazed up at Midnight, and then the cowboy saw the renegade scrabble in the mesquite and come up with a Colt and press the trigger.

His own guns were leaping into his hands, but he didn't fire because he remembered that he had only one round in them, and there was that Indian pony getting into the way as it rolled on to its feet again.

Felipe started to fire. Someone knocked Midnight down. It was a blow meant for his head, but it caught the cowboy on his shoulder and sent him spinning. His gun flew out of his hand — the gun with the one precious round in it. Sandy was screaming, back of him.

Dazed, he rolled over in the dust and looked up. A horse reared apparently

288

miles into the sky. The big, matted head of the Longhorn seemed to look down at him from an incredible height. Then Sandy's scream shrilled up again as those vicious hooves came stabbing down for his body.

Midnight rolled, just in time — rolled forward, too, a dangerous trick, but one a rodeo performer will pull off to get the crowd on its feet. For rolling forward put him out of the line of vision of horse and rider, momentarily.

He came round and up. Guns were blasting near by. Felipe was screaming as the slugs tore into his bare body. Midnight glimpsed the scrub-face that had been listening to their plans outside the office that day — saw two other faces just as rough and evil. They were Longhorn's gunnies, hired to help stir up trouble for the benefit of their big-city financier employers.

Felipe was sprawling, stretching out on his face, either dead or shamming. The three hombres, guns smoking, were coming round to deal with

Midnight, the man they had been ordered to wipe out.

Midnight rose up from the horse's belly and heaved on a stiff leg inside a stirrup. The Longhorn rose into the air and crashed to the ground. Midnight saw that one foot was still in the far stirrup, and punched with all his might into the horse's stomach. With a scream of fury it lashed out and then set off at a mad gallop across the prairie, and the thing that bumped and screamed alongside it served only to madden it further and keep it racing at its fastest.

Midnight was thinking, grimly, 'Waal, that's one less fer me to deal with,' and turned to look into the barrels of three guns. And there was no cover, no chance of escape. And the way they were looking, those hardened, callous professional gunmen didn't intend to let him escape.

The scrub-faced hombre's finger was whitening around the trigger. Then Felipe shot him.

Felipe was going out fast, but while

their backs were turned he had rolled painfully over on to his side. Right to the last he was a killer. He knew he was going to die, and he was determined to take as many as possible with him to the Happy Hunting Grounds.

Scrub-face didn't utter a sound, but just toppled from the saddle — and Midnight was right underneath. Then Felipe tried to pull his gun round on to other targets, but perhaps his eyes were bleary suddenly, for his shots went wide and missed, and the other men blasted the last spark of life out of the renegade simultaneously.

When they turned to do the same to Midnight, they found a grim-faced man looking at them across the saddle of Scrub-face's horse, and the blue bore of Scrub-face's gun was eyeing them balefully.

Midnight said, 'I'll open up sooner than you can,' and said no more.

They hesitated, recognising the truth of what he said, their own guns not yet pointing round at Midnight, and then, without any order from Midnight, they dropped their weapons and slowly raised their hands.

Sandy came swiftly across and scooped up their guns. Then she backed, a Colt supplementing Midnight's. She called, 'Guess I feel faint, Tom.' Then, frontierswoman that she was, she added, 'Reckon, though, I'll save it till we get back to the ranch-house.'

Big Tom said, 'Get off them hosses — an' walk. An' ef I ever catch you in Medina County again, I'll sure make holes the size o' peas through your hide.'

They got down reluctantly. Midnight mounted one of the horses and led the other away. They went off pretty quickly, so as not to give the pair time to find and reload a gun. And so they came to the carnage that was old man Ricketts' ranch.

But the fighting was over; victory had been won by the white men. And sitting and drinking in great harmony were the fence busters and Midnight's men. Their common enemy, the red man, had brought back the comradeship that in late months had largely departed.

★ ★ ★

Ricketts settled wearily in his chair. It had taken some hard work to clear up the ranch, but thanks to neighbourly assistance, it was in fair shape now. There was a queer look in his old eye; it could have been anger but it might have been humour.

'Tierney's called the ban off on barbed wire, Tom,' he announced abruptly.

All Midnight said was, 'That's considerate o' the fellar, mighty considerate.'

'Tierney knows he's licked. He knows he got in the wrong side, an' now he's playin' for fencers' sympathies. He reckons to stay on bein' sher'f no matter what happens.'

Midnight sighed. 'Yeah, I guess there

won't be no range war over wire, now. But I don't see Tierney wearin' a badge much longer. If he's got sav he'll sure take the back trails an' make fer places where he ain't known.'

They were silent, both thinking. Old man Ricketts broke the silence. 'The way I see it, Tom, you'll need some place to stock your wire when it starts comin' through. Oh, sure, I know you'll need an office back in town, but you ain't got no place there to take more'n a wagon-load. Now, here' — he indicated the many outbuildings to his ranch — 'here there's room for as much wire as you'd like to bring in.'

Midnight said, 'I don't get you, pardner?'

So Ricketts said, simply, 'I don't want you to leave me, Tom, you and Sandy. I'm an old man, an' I guess I like young people about. Come an' live with me here at the ranch — store your wire out here, ef you like. But don't — leave me, Tom.' His voice was wistful.

Midnight exclaimed, 'You'd really like me to?'

So Ricketts got testy, as he often did, and said, 'The hell, would I ask you ef I didn't?' Then he relaxed. 'Of course I do, son. You an' Sandy'll be gettin' married any time now; I guess it would be a kindness to an old man to have young company around. What say, Tom? Regard the place as yours as it will be some day, boy?'

Tom Midnight rose and went across to the old man. 'I'll take you, pardner,' he said. 'Guess we three sure can be happy on this spread for many a long year. Reckon I'll go tell the boys.' Then he paused. 'You know what, old-timer? While they were here no less'n five fence busters sneaked up an' started askin' things about wire. Guess I'm gonna make that fortune Uncle Walt promised.'

He went out on to the veranda. His men were all there — King Cass with his arm in a sling, Big Joe Culloch scowling from blackened eyes and a bandaged head, the Callason brothers both with bandages on their fists, Skippy Playfellow sitting with his foot in the air because of a wild treading horse in the mêlée, Mex with a stiffness to his walk that spoke of some smashing blow to the ribs. They were all there — even Wee Jock was leaning out of the window playing poker with some of the ranch men. All except old Deaf Ector.

Then Sandy came running up the steps to meet him. She said, 'I'm ready to go,' because they'd thought they would have to leave the ranch.

Midnight said, 'Let's go, honey. Reckon we'll be safe in Devine after the last shindig. Reckon we'll get married quick an' good, then come back here an' live for ever after, huh? That's how the old-timer wants it.'

And that's how it was.

Other titles in the
Linford Western Library:

THE GALLOWS GANG

I. J. Parnham

After escaping the gallows eight condemned men, led by Javier Rodriguez, blaze a trail of destruction, leaving swinging bodies as a reminder of the fate they'd avoided. Four men set out to bring them to justice: prison guards Shackleton Frost and Marshal Kurt McLynn; Nathaniel McBain, a man wrongly condemned himself and under suspicion from Frost and McLynn, and the enigmatic man known as The Preacher. Can this feuding, mismatched group end the Gallows Gang's reign of terror?